Lumberjack Under the Tree

Also by Keira Andrews

Contemporary

Honeymoon for One
Beyond the Sea
Ends of the Earth
Arctic Fire
The Chimera Affair

Holiday
The Christmas Deal
The Christmas Leap
Only One Bed
Merry Cherry Christmas
Santa Daddy
In Case of Emergency
Eight Nights in December
If Only in My Dreams
Where the Lovelight Gleams
Gay Romance Holiday Collection
Lumberjack Under the Tree (free read!)

Sports
Kiss and Cry
Reading the Signs
Cold War
The Next Competitor
Love Match
Synchronicity (free read!)

Gay Amish Romance Series
A Forbidden Rumspringa
A Clean Break
A Way Home

A Very English Christmas

Valor Duology
Valor on the Move
Test of Valor
Complete Valor Duology

Lifeguards of Barking Beach
Flash Rip
Swept Away (free read!)

Historical

Kidnapped by the Pirate
Semper Fi
The Station
Voyageurs (free read!)

Paranormal

Kick at the Darkness Trilogy
Kick at the Darkness
Fight the Tide

Taste of Midnight (free read!)

Fantasy

Barbarian Duet
Wed to the Barbarian
The Barbarian's Vow

Lumberjack Under the Tree

KEIRA ANDREWS

Lumberjack Under the Tree
Written and published by Keira Andrews
Cover by Dar Albert
Formatting by BB eBooks

Copyright © 2021 by Keira Andrews
Print Edition

Chapter One

Blake

I ALMOST DIDN'T recognize him with the beard.

To be fair, my first love was the last person on Earth I'd expected to encounter when my boss told me there was a new hire.

Standing by the flatbed truck, I couldn't breathe. I'd been sucker-punched once outside a bar, and this blow was worse. Apparently the feeling was mutual. Adam's apple bobbing, brown eyes wide, Caleb Walker gaped at me.

Caleb had been fit back in the day, and he'd filled out even more as an adult. His chestnut hair was thick and his beard trimmed close like mine. There was a drop of dried blood on his throat where he'd nicked himself.

My eyes locked on that spot, and I recalled sucking a hickey right about there, fledgling stubble under my tongue. My pulse zoomed as if I was about to do it again, my body remembering him far too vividly as my brain raced to catch up.

"What?" Nick demanded. "You two know each other?" He scratched his own dark beard.

"We don't." I nodded curtly to Caleb and stuck out my hand. "Blake Martin." It wasn't a lie precisely—I *didn't* know him. We were thirty now, and I hadn't laid eyes on Caleb since high school. It was ludicrous to think of him as my "first love." Give me a break. We'd messed around one night. Big deal.

"Uh, hi." Caleb pulled off his work glove and shook my hand for approximately a nanosecond. Was he afraid to touch me after all this time?

A sneer curled my lip, but I forced it into a smile as Hunter walked over from the farm's glass-fronted timber house holding a pair of crutches. He held them out to Nick and greeted Caleb.

"Welcome to Spini Farm! We spoke the other day. I see you've met Nick. I'm his cheerier half. Sorry if he's being a grump." He wiggled the crutches and gave Caleb a grin. "Nick's always a bit grumpy, TBH." Hunter was smooth-faced and in his mid-twenties, about half Nick's age.

Nick huffed, which honestly only proved Hunter right. "I can stand here just fine." His foot was in a cast housed in a plastic boot, and he leaned heavily on his right leg.

"Uh-huh. And you think I didn't see you hobbling over here? You'll just make it take longer to heal."

Hunter stubbornly held out the crutches until Nick snatched them up, putting them under his arms with a muttered curse.

I shared a smile with Hunter, trying to focus as my mind spun in overdrive. I glanced to my right, and yep. *Caleb Walker* was still standing there like a deer in headlights.

A strapping, bearded deer in faded jeans that hugged his lean thighs.

"Glad you're here, Caleb," Hunter said, shaking his hand. "Nick hates needing extra help around the farm, but he'll get used to it." He winked at Nick. "He always does."

Caleb nodded, eyes still wide. Did it make him uncomfortable that Nick and Hunter were a couple? Considering they were the bosses, he'd better get over it. Surely he'd dealt with his hang-ups by now. It'd been more than a decade since our little...*rendezvous.* It had been nothing. A blip.

My chest ached with bittersweet memories, my body stubbornly denying that it hadn't mattered. That *he* hadn't mattered.

Shivering, Hunter tugged a woolen toque over his blond hair. "Nearing December, and it finally feels like winter's coming, huh?" He nodded toward the barn. "I'm going to take down the last of the Halloween stuff in the rafters and string the lights for Santa's village next weekend. There'll be a ton of real cobwebs up there by now."

"Be careful," Nick said.

"Yes, dear." On tiptoe, Hunter kissed his hairy cheek. "Don't worry, I won't get startled by the dog and fall off the ladder."

"It wasn't the dog—it was her face full of porcupine quills!" Nick grumbled as Hunter headed to the barn with a cheeky wave. Nick watched him go, his prickly frown melting into a tiny, tender smile.

I ignored the spike of—was that *jealousy*? What the hell? Since when was I jealous of Hunter and Nick's odd-couple domestic bliss? I was just fine on my own. I loved the freedom to travel and do whatever I wanted. I had zero interest in settling down.

Nick turned his attention back to us, leaning on the crutches. "Blake, you know the job. Caleb, since you have harvesting experience, you can hit the ground running. Yes?"

"Absolutely," Caleb said hoarsely. He cleared his throat. "Yes."

Huh. He had experience harvesting trees? I thought he'd joined the military after going down to the States on that hockey scholarship. Not that I'd been keeping tabs on him. Clearly he wasn't enlisted now if he was out here near Pinevale doing seasonal work on a Christmas tree farm.

Nick nodded decisively. "Blake's in charge. You do what he tells you."

"Yes, sir," Caleb said.

A rogue bolt of desire stuttered my lungs because my

4

body was still not getting with the program. I needed to get laid if I was remotely turned on by Caleb Walker of all people. Time to stop acting like a baby duck that had imprinted on the first guy I fell for. Apparently the hundreds of times I'd jerked off in high school thinking of him had left more of a mark than I'd realized.

I did allow myself a moment of smug satisfaction that he'd have to answer to me. Not that there was much to the job, and he certainly had the muscles required…

Ordering myself to stop cataloging said muscles under his snug khaki field jacket, I asked Nick, "By the way, did the haunted house go well?"

"Yeah, surprising how many people are into that nonsense." Nick's face softened. "That's all Hunter's department. He loves trying new ideas to bring in revenue. He's the reason we're expanding our acreage. There'll be a lot of work next spring—all year round at this point if you change your mind about heading south after the holidays."

I laughed. "Van life's great, but the external shower is a lot more enjoyable in warm weather." Unease tugged through me, but I pushed it aside. Van life *was* great. Freedom! Flexibility! The open road! Nothing and no one to tie me down. It was exactly what I wanted.

Nick said to Caleb, "As I mentioned, there'll be lots of work in the future. We'll see how you get on the next few weeks. Follow Blake's orders and you'll do just fine." He peered toward the barn. "I should make sure Hunter's okay on that ladder." He grumbled. "Can't believe I let him talk me into expanding the holiday festival even more."

I laughed. "Poor ol' Grinch. Can't deny his man. And you know it's good for business."

With a grunt, Nick tossed me a set of keys. "Walkie-talkie's in the truck if you need me." He had the second radio squeezed into his back pocket. Nick was pushing fifty, but he still looked damn good in a pair of jeans and tight plaid shirt.

To Caleb, Nick added, "No cell signal this far from town, so if you're expecting messages, you're shit out of luck."

"No problem. I'll be too busy working to check my phone."

I barely resisted rolling my eyes at the brown-nosing, but Nick barked out a laugh. "That's what I like to hear." Muttering about the crutches, he left us to it.

We watched him go for a few awkward seconds. We were both around six foot, but Caleb hunched, his hands jammed in his pockets. Scuffing the toe of his spotless work boots in the dirt, he looked anywhere but at me.

He'd always been jittery, though he used to hide it better. He'd been captain of the hockey team and popular with everyone at school. But when you got to know him…

When you *got to know him, he was a coward who broke your heart.*

Oh, for fuck's sake. He hadn't *broken my heart*—that was ridiculously dramatic. I'd dated plenty of guys over the years. My heart was doing just fine.

Smiling carelessly, I said, "We should get to work."

"Right." Caleb nodded, and we climbed up into the truck. It was a handful, but not quite big enough that I needed a special license. I turned onto the dirt access road that wound through the farm.

"Um, so… What's this holiday festival all about?" Caleb asked.

"It's the three weekends before Christmas, partnering with Nadeau Family Farms nearby to encourage people to visit both. They produce maple syrup over there. Here, a few of the grids closer to the barn and main area are opened for folks to cut down their own trees. Sleigh rides, family activities, hot snacks. That kind of stuff. This year, there's a new Santa's village in the barn. There's a big fundraiser too during the last weekend— toys and turkeys."

"Sounds great." Caleb took off his gloves, then put them on again.

I turned down another fork of the service road that snaked farther out toward the distant ridge. Thick evergreens filled the undulating land. It really was a beautiful spot, and it had felt secret and special—my little retreat.

And now *Caleb Walker* was here.

Not that I cared, but… Curiosity won. "What are you doing out this way? You don't live in Barrie anymore?" Though the forty-five minute drive was certainly commutable.

Caleb made a strange little noise. "So you… You do remember me?" he asked. His voice was low and still hoarse like he needed a drink.

I smirked. "I remember you. For what it's worth." What did that even mean? I was being a dick, and I wasn't even sure why.

You know exactly why.

I gripped the worn steering wheel, hoping my gloves hid that I was white-knuckling it. This wasn't the plan. I was supposed to work my body hard, pick up some extra cash, and finish my latest book in a place with no Wi-Fi to tempt me with its endless distractions. Then head south for a few months and write the next book by the beach.

Toiling side-by-side with Caleb Walker was distraction on a whole new level.

Caleb simply said, "No, I'm not living in Barrie."

He didn't elaborate, which was fair enough. How bizarre to be sitting next to him. I'd never expected to see him again. Why would I? Aside from on Facebook, which I'd go weeks without checking, I hadn't stayed friends with anyone from high school. I sure as hell hadn't been friends with Caleb on social media.

Yeah, I'd looked him up once in a moment of weakness, and his profiles had been dormant. And maybe I'd spotted Melissa commenting on someone's post a few years ago and I'd combed through her profile to see if she and Caleb were still together.

And *fine*, I'd been grimly satisfied that she was married to a used car salesman with a big house in one of the new developments in the Barrie burbs where a person would be hard-pressed to walk between the houses without turning sideways.

"You don't live in Toronto anymore?" Caleb asked.

My stomach somersaulted. Had he kept tabs on me? "Nah. Got sick of the city." I was about to explain about my writing but stopped myself. I didn't owe Caleb Walker any explanations. But how did he end up *here?* With me? Screwing with my stress-free holiday plans?

He asked, "How did you become a lumberjack?"

Normally, I would have scoffed at that description and denied it. But hell, I *was* a lumberjack—at least temporarily. "I was Hunter's TA in university. Last year, he posted online about needing seasonal help." It'd been dumb luck that I'd seen his post, and I'd jumped at a new adventure and a place to park my van. "Can't beat the location."

We passed rows of fir and pine trees, the sections in different stages of growth. The land rolled to the horizon, a creek cutting through the low ground. Old-growth forest surrounded us.

I added, "Plus, it's a good workout. Who needs CrossFit?"

From the corner of my eye, I swear his gaze dragged low over my body. It was petty, but damn—that felt good. He could look all he wanted—he wasn't allowed to touch me again.

Whoa. Caleb touching me was a dangerous train of

thought, and I corralled it immediately. Besides, Caleb was now staring out his window. I'd imagined it. Which should not have made me squirm with disappointment.

He said, "Wow. So many trees. How long do they take to grow?"

"Depends. Around seven years is the average. Nick has a grid system that benefits the trees and soil." I paused. "I thought you had harvest experience?"

"I do! Just not with Christmas trees." He fiddled with his work gloves, tightening then loosening the strap on one wrist. "Didn't I hear that you're a writer?"

I shrugged nonchalantly. "Yeah. I'm working on the fifth book in a series. Traveling around in a van, turning my university side hustle into my career. Hitting every millennial cliché."

"In the books or your life?" he asked plainly.

I barked out a laugh. I remembered that about him—that he could be funny without intending it. "My life. Probably the books too."

Caleb smiled hesitantly, and goddamn it—there were those dimples. He'd had an endearing sincerity that had always made me—

No. Memory lane was officially closed to traffic.

Still, as I geared down and brought the truck to a stop, I found myself asininely asking, "What happened with Melissa?" It was a ludicrous question. It was ancient history.

"We tried long distance for a while when I went down to Wisconsin. But it didn't work out."

"Did you cheat on her again?"

He went rigid. Not looking at me, he shook his head stiffly and yanked open the door to jump down from the cab.

Ugh. Why had I said that? I'd been naive at the time for expecting East Barrie Secondary School's hockey star to break up with a popular, gorgeous girl for me. A fool back then and probably an asshole now to throw it in his face after twelve years.

Still behind the wheel, I sat there and debated apologizing until too much time had passed. Besides, we were here to work. I'd told Nick we didn't know each other, and that was the way it should be. Caleb's love life was none of my business. It never had been. Just because he was the guy I—

Oh, for fuck's sake. Don't go there. You got over Caleb Walker a long time ago.

We had a job to do, and it wasn't unearthing teenage betrayal.

Chapter Two

Caleb

FOR A SECOND, I'd been so freaking happy to see him.

Which was stupid because Blake had stared at me like I was dog shit stuck to the bottom of his boot. But that first breath when I realized the gorgeous man I'd be working with was actually, really, honest-to-god *Blake Martin* all grown?

A balloon of happiness had lifted me up, up, up—then *splat*. Back to earth. Down into the ditch.

I followed him around the small clearing. Pointing to a red-painted machine he called a baler, Blake gave short bursts of instructions—not angry, just to the point. Businesslike, you could say. I'd follow his orders and try not to screw up. In the meantime, I tried not to stare.

Did I mention he was gorgeous? Lean muscles and blond hair and facial scruff. Those blue eyes. Before I'd ruined everything, those eyes had looked at me with so much kindness. They'd crinkled at the corners when he laughed.

For that incredible second when I'd made him laugh again, the crinkles had fanned out maybe a bit farther than they used to. Freckles dusted the tops of his cheeks, and I could imagine them darker with a summer tan.

And he *did* remember me.

The idea that he'd erased what happened between us like a factory reset on a phone had knocked the wind out of me. Shaking his hand had been like the time as a kid when I'd leaned on the stove without realizing the burner was on. That stupidity had left me with a coiled scar on my palm. I imagined even now that it throbbed a warning to not be an idiot.

Blake opened a crate on the back of the truck and lifted out a black and yellow chainsaw. My gut clenched. "We're not using axes?" I asked before I could bite my tongue.

His forehead creased. "Ha-ha."

It hadn't been a joke, but I tried to laugh. We used to laugh so much together. That was one of the things I'd missed most about Blake. Laughing about nothing and everything.

I eyed the chainsaw. I knew how to use an ax. The cottage had a wood-burning stove, and my dad had given me the chore of wood-chopping when I was young. I'd had plenty of practice lately.

That was breaking up logs, not chopping down trees,

but I'd been sure I could pick it up quickly enough to fake it until I made it. I should have known a Christmas tree farm would use chainsaws.

Dread sank through me, my face going hot. I had to admit I had no clue how to use a chainsaw. But Blake was holding one out for me, so I took it, not surprised that it weighed a good fifteen pounds or more.

The smell of gas stung my nose, and I watched carefully as Blake filled his saw before passing me the red plastic can. The whole time I filled my tank, I examined the controls. It didn't look too complicated. How hard could it be?

After I screwed the cap back on the gas tank, Blake tossed me an orange helmet, clear plastic goggles, and a little plastic container with orange foam earplugs stuffed inside. I squeezed one flat and twisted it into my ear, then the other.

Of course Blake started talking, and all I could hear was a murmur and my own rapid heartbeat. I pulled out the earplugs, hoping my beard covered my blush as I asked, "What was that?"

Blake popped an eyebrow. "Do I have your attention now?"

"Yes, sir."

He went very still, and I was desperate for the ground to open and swallow me. I hadn't meant to say that. I'd called Nick Spini "sir," but that made sense. He was a stranger, older than me, and the owner of the farm. Would Blake think I was mocking him?

I quickly added, "I just mean—yes. I'm listening. Sorry, I did a couple tours in the army, and it's hard to break the habit." Then I dropped one of the bits of orange foam with my clumsy fingers and bent to pick it up from the dirt.

Just don't drop the chainsaw.

I had to focus. Without this job, I was up shit's creek without a canoe. Forget about a paddle.

Blake marched away. "Time to get to work. We'll start with that row of firs. Cut the row first, then through the baler."

My heart thumped even louder thanks to the earplugs. I could do this. I watched Blake power through the first tree. Seemed straightforward. He didn't look like he was paying attention to me.

Holding down the rear handle with my boot, the chainsaw on the ground, I pulled the cord the way he had, also adjusting the choke. I knew enough about engines to get the basic mechanics. The engine turned over and roared to life after another tug of the cord.

I picked it up, the saw vibrating. Even with the earplugs, it was *loud.* Like handling a wild animal with its fangs out. This was stupid. This was dangerous. But could I ask him for help? Or would it cost me this job on the very first day?

Why did it have to be *him*? Of all the people on Earth, he was the one I'd ached to see. The one I wanted to make amends with. The one I never wanted to disappoint again. I felt like a dumb kid, terrified of screwing everything up and making it worse by staying silent. But I wasn't a kid. I could do this. I *would* do this.

Engine whirring, I bent, braced, and lowered the saw to the trunk, squeezing the throttle with my right fingers and—

"Stop!"

Rearing back, I killed the engine and blinked through the goggles. "Huh?"

"You almost hit the tip!" Blake yanked down his goggles, and they swayed on a cord around his neck. "What the hell are you doing?"

After putting down the chainsaw gratefully, I pulled out the ear plugs and removed the goggles. I felt like I was back in school and hadn't studied for an exam. "Cutting down the tree?"

Hands on hips, Blake glared. "You may look the part of a lumberjack, but you don't know what you're doing, do you? 'Harvesting experience' my ass."

Not only was there no point in lying—I didn't want to. Especially not to him. Not again. "I can use an ax, but no. I have no clue what I'm doing."

"Why are you here?" He held out his gloved hands. "Why *here*?"

"I need the job. I fudged my experience."

"Wonderful. Big talk and no follow-through. Sounds familiar." Blake opened his mouth, then snapped it shut. "Forget it. Look, I only learned last year from Nick. It's not rocket science." His gaze ran down my body. "You've got the strength for it. But the kickback on one of these heavy-duty chainsaws can take off your head if you don't know what you're doing."

"Can you teach me?" I cleared my throat. "*Will* you teach me?"

In the distance, a dog barked. I hoped it wasn't poking another porcupine. Holding my breath, I waited to see whether I'd end up with a face full of quills from Blake.

"I should go tell Nick and Hunter this isn't going to work. Cut our losses." His nostrils flared, his lips pressing into a tight line.

"If you give me a chance, I won't let you down." I shook my head. "Let *them* down, I mean."

He was silent a few moments. "Guess you didn't become a hockey star."

I had to laugh. "No way. After I blew out my knee freshman year in Wisconsin, they cut me loose. I was never good enough for the NHL anyway. Joined CAF since I didn't know what else to do."

He frowned. "Is that…Canadian Armed Forces?"

"Right. I left last year when my dad got sick."

Blake's frown deepened, his mouth turning down. "Sorry to hear it. Is he…?"

"Gone. Don't have much family. You remember my mom died before we met."

"Yeah. The government must give you benefits if you had an honorable discharge or whatever they call it?"

I nodded. "It's not much, though. Dad had some debt I had to deal with. Things are tight. I've been looking everywhere for a few months now." My throat was too dry. "I need this."

For too long, Blake was silent. Then he strapped on his goggles. "Okay. Starting at the beginning."

Sighing in relief, I secured my goggles and helmet, leaving the earplugs in my pocket so I could hear his instructions as he explained the anatomy of the chainsaw and how to start it. I followed along, and after a dry run, I picked up the running saw.

"Never touch anything with the tip of the saw, especially the top of the tip."

It sounded kinda dirty, but I was probably just horny. I mean, I was *definitely* horny, but I had to focus. "Got it."

Blake picked up his saw, which was still off. He widened his stance and mimed sawing into the trunk of the tree he'd felled as if he was shortening it. "If you use the tip, it can kick back up toward your face." He pretended to saw with the tip and suddenly yanked the chainsaw up.

"Wow!" Now I could see how the force could kick it up like stepping on a rake.

"At full throttle that can be deadly. When we're cutting down trees, even if it didn't hit your face because of the side angle, it could yank you off your feet and still do serious damage."

Shit. No wonder he'd yelled at me. "Got it."

Blake took a step closer before jerking to a stop. "Left hand in front. Thumb wrapped around the upper handle—that's important. Arm straight and elbow locked. That flap there in front of the bar is your emergency brake. Push it forward with your left wrist, and it stops the chain. Right hand on the rear handle. Keep that arm bent a little. Good." He nodded toward the line of firs.

The air was clear and crisp, and right next to the trees, it was like breathing in a Christmas candle. Behind me, Blake half-shouted, "Don't stand right behind the chainsaw. To the left. Spread your legs."

Those three words made me hard.

Shit. I knew I was lonely, but… *Shit.* Face hot, I did as I was told, reminding myself I was holding a deadly saw and that this wasn't a jerk-off fantasy. I prayed my jacket covered me enough.

"You can get on your knees if you want."

Not. Helping.

I dropped to my left knee, my jeans painfully tight against my dick.

"Since we're cutting from the side, shift your left hand to the side bar and turn the saw. Yep, just like that. You're going to press the throttle with your right index finger and cut straight across with the middle of the blade. Firm, steady pressure."

Everything sounded dirty, but I nodded seriously, memorizing his instructions.

"The other cause of kickback is a pinched chain. Say if you stop mid-cut and the weight of the tree presses down and grips the chain. It can shove the chainsaw back toward you with the reactive force. Or jerk you forward or to the side right off your feet. These heavy-duty chainsaws are no joke."

"Right. Absolutely!" We had to practically shout to be heard, and the chainsaw in my hands did not feel even a little like a joke.

With my finger on the throttle and muscles tensed, I pushed the saw through the fir's trunk, the tree toppling and scattering dry scrub. I released the motor and stood, pulse racing as I looked to Blake for approval. Approval I shouldn't want so damn much.

He nodded. "Not bad! Cut's angled, though."

"Shit." I'd thought I was going straight, but… Story of my life, apparently. I snorted, quickly coughing when Blake frowned my way.

"It's easy to fix. Cut the bottom again, then do the next one."

One by one, I worked down the line of firs, Blake shadowing me and giving corrections. Then we hauled the trees to the baler and fed them through, the machine wrapping the trees in twine.

Though the breeze was chilly, sweat dampened the nape of my neck. Blake took off his jacket, and I tried not to stare at how his red, blue, and white plaid shirt clung to his long, lean torso. He'd said I looked the part of a lumberjack, but *damn.* So did he.

It was still hard to believe this was Blake. All grown up and helping me even though I didn't deserve it. When he nodded in approval as I put a tree through the baler on my own, pride and satisfaction flowed through me like a drug.

There was so much I wanted to say to him. For so long. Here was my chance, but where could I even start? As we took a break, sitting on the back of the truck eating our bagged lunches, I tried to come up with the perfect words. But words had been Blake's thing.

Finally, I just said, "Thank you for your help," then took another bite of my peanut butter sandwich.

Shrugging, he bit into an apple with a crunch. "We've got a job to do." After finishing the apple and checking his watch, he balled up the foil from his sandwich and tossed it back into an insulated lunch bag. "Speaking of which." He shoved his earplugs back in.

That was it for the rest of the afternoon. At least the hours sped by, and I enjoyed the rhythm of the work. After months of job hunting, it felt damn good to do something productive.

On the silent, weird drive back up the service road in the late afternoon, I spotted a big white van down by the creek. I had to know. "Is that yours? You said something about living in a van?"

"Yeah. My dad's a contractor. He helped me fix it up. Taught me a lot."

"Awesome. I remember that about your dad. Looks like a cool ride."

"We do all right traveling around."

Wait. Did he mean *we* as in…him and the van? Or his dad, maybe? Or… I looked back, squinting to see if anyone was in the vehicle. It didn't look like lights were on, but it was too far to know for sure.

Did he have a boyfriend? A husband? A partner? Whatever you wanted to call it—did Blake have a man?

No reason he shouldn't, I reminded myself. Even though he hadn't been fully out in high school, his family had known, and he'd been very confident that he was gay. It had taken me years to get there, as much as I'd wanted to be with him. As much as I'd wanted to be brave.

No reason he shouldn't have a man, and no reason for me to feel kicked in the gut with jealousy. Also, hadn't I decided when I came home from my last tour overseas and got my honorable discharge that I was going to be honest?

I'd finally come out, and it hadn't been nearly as scary as I'd built it up to be. I could ask Blake if he was dating someone.

"Who's we?" I blurted. Real smooth.

Eyes on the road, Blake said, "Me and Herman."

Herman? Maybe he was older? Was it like Nick and Hunter? Although Herman sounded like a senior citizen. "Uh…" I sucked with words.

"My van. My white whale. Not in the sense of an all-consuming quest for vengeance. Just in that it's big and white. I call him Herman."

"Oh!" It rang a faint bell from grade twelve English class. "*Moby-Dick?*"

"Not very original, I know. But Herman's perfect for

van life. I moved back in with my parents for six months, and we fixed him up. Solar panels on the roof for power, mini fridge, induction hot plate. Toilet. Not one of those ultra-luxury vans you see on Instagram, but it does me."

"That's great. Just, uh—just you?"

The air got thick, Blake's jaw clenching. His voice was tight. "Yep. Just me."

"Great," I repeated. Wait, was that a dumb thing to say? "I mean… Um…"

"What about you? No wife? Girlfriend?" He asked so sharply it made me think of the chainsaw cutting into wood.

"No." I fiddled with my seatbelt, which was about to strangle me. It locked, and I had to release it to get more slack before doing it up again. The *click* sounded too loud in the silence over the steady rumble of the truck's engine.

Be brave.

"I'm gay. It took me a long time to accept it and everything. But I am. And I'm glad."

Blake slanted a look at me. His voice dropped—loosened?—into his smooth, normal way of talking. "Okay. That's good. Are you…" He cleared his throat. "Seeing anyone?"

I shook my head. "I hooked up with guys once I lost my scholarship and enlisted." I added firmly, "After I'd broken up with Mel." I'd cheated on her with Blake that one night, and I never, ever did it again. "But when I came back to look after my dad, there was too much going on."

Eyes still front, he said, "Right. I get it."

I realized I'd tensed my whole body as I managed a deep breath. There. I'd done it. When I'd woken too early that morning, worrying about impressing my new boss, I'd never thought in a million years that it would be Blake. That I'd get the chance to tell him I'd come out. It was a relief but also exciting. Scary but exciting.

But why? It wasn't like I had a second chance with Blake. Unless… No way. Forget it. I couldn't let myself even think it.

I said, "I guess you can park it anywhere if there's solar power. You don't have to be in an RV park or wherever." In the silence, I added, "Herman, I mean."

Still not looking at me, he nodded. "Some campgrounds are way too crowded."

"Right." After a few awkward moments, I asked, "How are they doing? Your family?"

"Great." He seemed glad of the change of subject. "My brother and my older sister Kristen are both married with kids. Sara's finishing up university and heading to teachers' college."

"Wow." I smiled. "I can't believe she's that big. I still think of her as ten and begging you to let her play Nintendo."

Blake exhaled, almost grinning, then frowning as if remembering he wasn't supposed to smile around me. He'd been a typical dickhead older brother to Sara, telling her to scram. But I'd usually given her my controller and coached her on how to beat him. I'd been so jealous that Blake had siblings.

He was still frowning. Worry tapped me on the shoulder, and I asked, "Sara's doing okay, right?"

"Huh? Oh, yeah. She's great! I was thinking about—" He pressed his lips together, shifting restlessly behind the wheel before blurting, "Black water."

I tried to remember where I'd heard that name. "The…mercenaries in the States?"

"What? Oh! No. Not them. The tank on my van. I need to empty it. The toilet water."

"Ah." *Okaaaay.*

He smiled tightly. "The realities of van life. Black water is from the toilet and gray water is from the sink. The farm's on a septic system, so I can dump them directly. There's a PVC pipe in the ground by the house. Tall orange flag on it so I can find it if it snows. Anyway."

Blake was speaking fast and fidgeting. Was he…*nervous*? What did he have to be nervous about? I was the one trying to impress him. He was in charge.

I shifted, the truck's leather squeaking. I couldn't start thinking of Blake taking charge in other ways. Not allowed.

We both fidgeted, and I asked, "How are your parents?" too loudly.

"Good. Great. They took early retirement. Semi, at least. Dad'll probably be working until he's dead. But they're wintering down in Florida now. I'll visit when I go south."

"Cool. Seems pretty isolated here?"

"Exactly what I'm looking for. It's only a few kilometers from the main house along the creek. But we all have our privacy."

In the twilight, the big windows of the house glowed warmly as we came over a rise. I imagined Hunter and Nick inside, cooking dinner maybe. They were so lucky to have each other and such an amazing place to live. I breathed through the longing. Maybe one day.

We hopped out of the truck, and I extended my hand. "Thanks." Wait. That wasn't enough. "You were the last person I thought I'd find here, but it's good to see you anyway." There was probably a far better way to say it, but too late now.

Blake seemed to want to say something. But he blew out a long breath and shook my hand, grasping it too tightly for a second before letting go. "You're welcome. Look, we've got three weeks of work until the big Christmas event weekend on the twentieth. Let's just get the job done. We don't have to be friends. Or enemies. Just…" He waved a hand. "Coworkers."

"Yep. See you in the morning." I hurried to my pickup, cringing at the *creak* as I opened the door and climbed up. I shoved in the key and prayed the son of a bitch engine would turn over.

It sputtered before catching, and I slumped against the cracking leather. As I headed out on the driveway, I could see Blake's lean silhouette in the rear-view mirror.

He was walking past the house, presumably to his van.

As I drove along the winding dirt driveway and eventually the two-lane highway back toward civilization, the radio played "Santa Claus is Comin' to Town." There was no snow yet, but it was definitely in the air.

I passed the Pinevale arena on my way to Home Depot, and it was ablaze with Christmas lights and snowmen decorations. The LCD sign flashed with the words:

MEN'S PICK-UP HOCKEY WED & SAT

On the passenger-side floor, my skates stared at me accusingly. I muttered, "Shut up," because I talked to skates now. I'd been meaning to check out the pick-up games for a few weeks now. Or months.

But this wasn't the time. I finally had a job, and it could lead to more. Maybe something permanent. If only. I needed this. I had to keep my head down and work. Hockey could wait. It wasn't a big deal. I'd try it later.

After picking up insulated work gloves and holding my breath as the purchase went through, I munched on a hot dog from the stand in the Home Depot parking lot. The hot, greasy meat was delicious, and I was glad I'd gotten fries too. I spilled a blob of ketchup on my leg and swiped at it with my finger.

The lane to the cottage was overgrown, branches scraping the sides of my truck like bony fingers. I laughed to myself as I arrived and switched off the engine. Halloween was over, and there were no ghosts out in these woods. I pulled the key out and the radio went silent, the dashboard lights fading. I switched off the headlights, and the night settled in.

The cottage sat dark, the expanse of the lake beyond. Through the bare trees, lights from a few neighbors shone in the distance, including strings of colored holiday bulbs. Most of the cabins around this lake were only used in the summer, but there were a handful of year-rounders. None of the nearby neighbors though, so they were just anonymous lights or curls of smoke in the dawn sky.

I should have introduced myself once I moved in before summer, and now it seemed too late even though it probably wasn't. I wondered if the cottages with holiday lights had trees up inside already.

When I was a kid, we'd always waited until mid-December, but my dad had been a bit of a Scrooge. I smiled to think of it. He was always the first to say it even though he crammed a ton of presents under the tree every year for Mom and I. After she passed, we hadn't bothered with any decorating or traditions, and I'd been overseas more often than not.

I was struck with a memory of our tree with the angel almost grazing the ceiling—Dad hoisting Mom up, his big hands around her waist so she could place the angel while I clapped. I still had that golden angel wrapped in old newspaper in one of the boxes in the dusty shed.

Inhaling deeply, I refocused on the dark wooden building in front of me. "Just sitting in my truck like a stalker," I muttered. Hey, at least I was outside my own house and not anyone else's. *House* was a wild exaggeration. Cabin/cottage/glorified shack was more like it.

My parents had loved this one-bedroom cottage, and I was grateful to have inherited it since the house in Barrie had gone toward debts and the cost of Dad's care home near the end.

I'd loved this place too as a kid, not minding that it was just the basics, living here in the summers and spending weekends all year long, sleeping on the old saggy couch with springs poking my butt.

My house. My home. I laughed, my breath clouding as the cold night set in, the truck's half-hearted heat faded now that I'd been sitting here for too long. My "home" was empty and dark and looked like it belonged in Hunter's Halloween thingy. But it had electricity and running water and an okay bed, and that had to be enough.

Maybe I wouldn't mind it so much if someone was waiting inside. Or if I had a Christmas tree with presents underneath. I scoffed. Who would buy *me* presents? Who would I buy for? I'd lost touch with my old friends a long time ago, and no one from the armed forces had really stuck. Tons of acquaintances, but no true *friends.* And definitely not anything more.

Scrunching my hot dog wrapper into the empty fry box, I climbed out, not bothering to lock the truck. No one was out here to swipe my skates or hockey pads. I should have brought them back inside and admitted that I was too shit-scared to do something as simple as join in a hockey game as an out gay man.

Soon. I'd go, and I'd tell people who I really was, and… Well, I guess I'd find out how they'd react. Blake, Nick, and Hunter all seemed to be doing fine in Pinevale. No reason to expect homophobia.

My teeth chattering something fierce, I got the fire going inside. The wood-burning stove heated the cottage far faster and cheaper than the electric baseboards. Winter really was coming to town. Too bad there was no Santa Claus to tag along.

Chapter Three

Blake

WHO NEEDED AN alarm when I had a raging erection to wake me?

It was still dark outside the van's windows, the days getting shorter and shorter. I braved sticking my hand out from under my thick duvet to grab my phone and blink at the screen. No signal out here, but it worked as an alarm clock.

Hell. Only ten minutes until I had to get up, so no point in going back to sleep. It would be hard anyway. Since I was hard.

"How witty. Aren't I supposed to be a writer? And when did I start talking to myself?"

Tugging the duvet back up to my neck, I shifted onto my back. The van's heater ran on the batteries powered by the solar panels, and I turned it down before bed the way I would a thermostat at home.

Well, *this* was my home. The way I would in a house or apartment. When would I get used to thinking of the van as home? Any day now. It wasn't that I disliked it, but…

"Oh, fuck," I muttered as I gave in and shoved my hand down my long johns to fondle my balls.

Every morning the past week, I'd tried valiantly not to think of Caleb Walker. I'd tried to ignore my straining dick and go about my morning routine like usual. I'd woken with an erection a million times since I was a horny kid. It hadn't been a big deal as an adult.

But for the past week since Caleb had burst back into my life, I'd careened out of control. He'd exploded back into my head. Into my traitorous subconscious that dreamed of him. Into my bloodstream that flooded its resources south to wake me pent up and craving release.

Craving *him.*

"Fuck that. Not happening."

But I couldn't stop touching myself. I shimmied down in my warm cocoon so I could spit into my palm. No need for lube when I was already so close to the edge, the remnants of dreams swirling through my head like fat snow flurries.

Caleb dropping to his knees, his beard rough on my inner thighs. Caleb bent over some object, begging for my cock. Wait, had that been a table of watermelons? Had I dreamed we were in the produce section at Foodland?

I spread my thighs, digging my heels into the firm

mattress as I stroked my straining shaft. Didn't matter where it happened—I was lost in the fantasy of burying my cock inside him while he surrendered and pleaded for more.

The only time we'd hooked up in real life, I'd sucked him, and we'd rubbed off, kissing so frantically I cut my lip. Now, I'd kiss him long and slow, our beards rubbing like kindling for a fire before I fucked his mouth, spit dribbling from his lips as he gulped and moaned.

It wasn't going to happen. Fantasies were harmless. Safe.

I twisted my nipples with my free hand in my co-coon of warmth under the duvet. I didn't know why my mind was intent on making Caleb submissive. Maybe it was the way he was so determined to please as we cleared acres of trees, following my instructions to a T and so transparently eager for my approval.

Pulling back my foreskin, I thumbed the head of my leaking dick, muscles bunching as I strained for release. Why shouldn't I imagine Caleb begging for my favor in bed too? It was all in my mind. Harmless. Safe.

As much as I tried to resist thinking of him at all, once I gave in it was an unstoppable flood.

Fucking his ass so hard he could only whimper. Taking him to the edge with my fingers, denying him my cock until I'm about to explode. Making him beg. Making him mine—

"Fuck!" I rubbed myself faster, rocking up in my grip, squeezing my nipple as I imagined coming in

Caleb's ass. His mouth. All over his face until it dripped from his beard.

I let myself cry out as the orgasm tore free. Shaking with waves of burning pleasure, I arched like a bow, cupping my hand over my cock to catch the hot splashes.

Caleb took every drop gratefully in my mind, and why shouldn't he? Why shouldn't I imagine dominating him? I'd steadfastly locked him out of my fantasies for years. It didn't mean anything to give in now.

Even if my mind was an asshole that produced images of tenderness too—*nuzzling Caleb's bristly cheek, whispering that he's good, sucking him off as he clutches my hair, so needy for me…*

"Not happening!"

I threw back the duvet and shot to my feet, wincing at the icy laminate floor on my bare feet and hopping into my fuzzy moccasins. No matter how cold it got, I hated sleeping in socks. My toes needed to be free.

You know what else needed to be free? My mind from these nonstop thoughts of Caleb. My body wasn't complaining about how satisfying the orgasms had been, but I had to get this under control. I was supposed to be writing in my down time, not taking this trip down memory lane.

Yet I'd barely written a few thousand words all week. I'd given myself a break on waking up an hour early to sprint, when I'd let the words flow without stopping to second-guess. But I wasn't sprinting at night either. I was half-heartedly poking at the chapters already written and putting my imagination to work wondering about Caleb's life.

And of course replaying that one night we'd shared. Well, more like an evening since I'd had to sneak out of his room in the middle of the night.

I'd had sex with my fair share of guys since then. Slept whole nights with plenty. Had relationships with some. Certainly had more competent sex than the one time with Caleb when neither of us knew what we were doing.

So why was that experience seared into my mind? Why did those sloppy, nose-bumping kisses make me want so much more? Why was fumbling with Caleb memory lane's greatest hit?

I'd blown through the ROAD CLOSED barrier like an out-of-control semi. Memory lane had become a highway of helpless lust.

"What even is this metaphor? Great work, *writer.*"

In disgust, I turned on the tap and scrubbed my hands and face in cold water. Two more weeks until Caleb and I parted ways and he returned to…wherever.

Where is *he living? What's he going to do for work in the new year? Will Nick and Hunter hire him on? If I come back next holiday, will he be here?*

Switching on the hot plate, I heated the kettle and scooped coffee grounds into the press I attached to the top of my travel mug. I wasn't a coffee snob but the quality really wasn't bad. A hell of a lot better than the instant stuff.

The window over the sink and hot plate steamed, and I pulled up the blinds and swiped it with my palm. The sun wasn't up yet, but I realized belatedly that the ground was unnaturally bright. Guess I'd been distracted by my dick. Pulling back the curtain between the living area and the two front seats, I groaned.

My walk to the flatbed truck's parking spot by the barn this morning was going to be through a foot of snow. It wasn't falling now, so the highway should be okay for Caleb to get in, depending on where he was coming from.

I poured the boiled water over the tube and stirred before pressing down the plunger slowly. He'd said he didn't live in Barrie. Pinevale was the closest town to us, so maybe he'd gotten a place there.

Of course I could just *ask* him all the questions that were piling up. But it wasn't like I actually cared. It was idle curiosity. It was to be expected, and none of it mattered. Caleb and I were coworkers doing a job. Nothing to see here.

End of story.

I CHECKED MY watch again in the gray light. Eleven minutes after eight. Caleb had been early every other day, but the roads were surely slow.

"Morning," Hunter said as he yawned widely, shuffling over in big boots and a puffy coat, his hat pulled down low. He followed my gaze to the mouth of the driveway through the forest. Snow pillowed the evergreens. "He's not late yet." Hunter laughed softly, like there was a private joke. "Not in my books, at least."

"Right. It's fine."

"No need to worry."

I scoffed and gulped from my mug, banging my teeth on the plastic. "Definitely not."

And sure enough, Caleb's beater of a pickup rattled around the bend, Caleb driving too fast for my liking. He wouldn't do any of us any good if he crashed, and I was glad to see him park safely.

Hunter said, "The guy who plows the lane and the service road will be here this morning, but I think the flatbed should be fine to get through this in the meantime. You're out on the far grid today?"

I nodded. "I'm still shocked Nick agreed to give up the plowing himself."

"Me too." He grinned wickedly. "But I have my ways."

Ella the beagle flew out of the house to investigate Caleb's arrival, barking loudly and tail wagging so hard it was amazing she didn't hurt herself. I watched Caleb crouch in the fresh snow and scratch behind her ears.

He'd had a dog growing up. A cute old mutt. It'd had an amusingly human name like "John" or "Steven." Did he have a dog now? He was speaking to Ella, his low voice soothing even though I couldn't make out the words. He petted her rhythmically with his bare hand, stroking up and down her back tenderly.

"She's back to normal after the porcupine incident?" I asked Hunter.

"Yep." He whistled to her, and she bounded over, ears flying. "Nick's not so great, though. I need to talk to you about it."

"Shit. His foot?"

"Afraid so. He's the worst patient." Hunter gave Ella a treat from his pocket and greeted Caleb.

"Sorry I'm late. The roads were slick." His words tumbled out anxiously.

"No problem." Hunter winced, half laughing. "Trust me, I know how treacherous winter driving can be. Speaking of which, Nick and I need to go to Toronto. His foot seems to be getting worse—probably because he's so stubborn about the crutches. He saw the doctor yesterday, and he referred Nick to a specialist. There's a cancellation for tomorrow morning, so we need to drive down this afternoon and stay in a hotel. There's more snow coming tonight, and the highways will be a shit show tomorrow."

I nodded. "Good plan. We can hold down the fort."

"Sweet, thanks. Do you mind watching Ella? You're welcome to stay in the guest room, of course."

The thought of a hot shower—with actual water pressure—was damn appealing. "I think I'll take you up on that." Ella rubbed my shins, and I bent to scratch her. "We'll have fun, won't we, girl?"

Hunter squinted up at the gray sky. "Be careful out

there. They're calling for possible snow squalls. You know how easy it is to get lost in a whiteout, so please knock off early if you need to. Caleb, be careful getting home. You're more than welcome to stay the night too if need be."

Caleb's gaze darted to me. "Oh, I'm sure I'll be fine. But thanks. Sorry about Nick's foot."

Hunter sighed. "Me too. It's hurting a lot. Partly because he hates admitting any weakness and is too stubborn to rest. He's elevating it right now, which means the pain is *intense*. I'm going to work on Santa's Village in the barn for a few hours, and then we'll get on the road."

Caleb asked, "Can we help?"

"No, but thank you. Harvesting takes priority. The demand will skyrocket this weekend now that it's finally snowing. I'd better get going. Santa won't have a throne to sit on otherwise."

"Who's playing Santa for the festival?" I asked.

Hunter grinned. "Who do you think?"

"No way." I sputtered. "*Nick*?"

"Yep. It's how we met, actually." He winked at me and Caleb. "I was a very naughty elf."

I laughed. "That tracks."

Caleb fidgeted, looking at his boots. Was he blushing?

Hunter added, "Good thing Santa can sit with his cast. Though if he's in too much pain, we might need one of you to pinch hit. Several days until Saturday, so we'll see. Would either of you be game?"

Before I could answer, Caleb said, "Of course. Anything you need."

More brown-nosing, but I supposed I couldn't begrudge him since he clearly wanted this temp gig to become permanent. Didn't matter to me. I'd be off down south, just me and Herman. Alone and free to write. I'd left the last book on a particularly evil cliffhanger, and my readers would be pissed if I delayed much longer.

No reason at all to think of Caleb staying on here without me with…what? Jealousy? Longing?

C) None of the above

I lifted my hands. "All yours. I'll supervise the tree cutting as planned." He was probably better with kids than I was.

I refocused as Hunter asked me, "You've got the spare key? Thanks for watching Ella. She should stay out of your hair once the chainsaws come on. Let's hope she doesn't find another porcupine den."

There were still a few marks on Ella's face from the quills, but she was tongue-waggingly thrilled to ride in the truck out to the far reaches of the farm. She sat on Caleb's lap in the passenger seat, happy as a pig in poop, as my mom would say.

"What was your dog's name?" I blurted. It was a safe enough topic.

For a moment, Caleb seemed about to look around to make sure I was talking to him and not a phantom passenger. Then he said, "Paul."

"That's it! I was thinking 'John' maybe."

"No, Dad's favorite Beatle was definitely Paul." Caleb hesitated, still petting Ella, who turned her head to lick his hand. "I don't know if you remember, but my dad was older when they had me. There was a fairly big age difference. Mom teased him about loving that sixties music he'd grown up with."

"The Beatles are timeless."

He looked at me, dimples pitting his cheeks. "That's what Dad said!"

"A wise man, clearly." I'd smiled back, and now I sighed. "Sorry he's not here anymore."

"It's okay." Caleb winced. "I mean… You know what I mean."

I nodded.

"Once I've got a steady job, maybe I'll get a dog." He nuzzled Ella. "Can't leave a puppy home alone, though."

"You need a boyfriend."

Did I just say that? *Out loud*?

I'd taken off my gloves once the warm air had started blasting from the vents, and now my knuckles were white on the steering wheel. "I just mean to look after the dog." I pried one hand loose and grabbed my coffee, gulping and finding it empty.

Caleb watched me, his gaze hot on my cheek. I fiddled with the heater, sweat suddenly dampening my hair under my wool hat. So much for *safe*. I shouldn't have mentioned the old dog. But I'd wanted to know. Not really about the dog—about…everything.

We hit a rut, the truck bouncing violently. I took my foot off the gas. "Whoa. I bet those muddy tire grooves are frozen now." The snow covered everything in a deceptively peaceful mantle.

Ella barked as if in agreement, and Caleb and I laughed weakly. We mercifully reached the work site a minute later, and I said, "Good thing we put the tarp over the baler when we moved it here yesterday. Don't want too much snow in the gears." I wasn't sure what I was even talking about, but it was work-related, so I went with it.

Soon enough, Ella frolicked in the snow, and we settled into the rhythm of the job. We'd established a routine over the past week of each of us taking a row, working our way down methodically. We'd cut the trees away from each other so there was no risk of being hit by one.

I reached the end of my row, and I watched Caleb go down on one knee and cut through the last trunk on his. He handled the chainsaw like a pro at this point, which made me strangely proud.

He released the throttle and stood, killing the engine and leaving the chainsaw on the bed of pine needles revealed by the felled tree. He took out his earplugs.

Without speaking, we began the next step of the process. These pines were tall—a good twelve feet. Standing on either side, we hoisted the tree by its trunk and shook off any dead needles.

We dragged the tree past its fallen comrades to where the baler waited, then fed it through. It was steady, heavy work, and aside from Ella returning every so often to bark suspiciously at the baler and get underfoot, it was business as usual.

Usual. How bizarre to step back and think about how quickly I'd gotten used to having Caleb in my life again.

I scoffed. *In my life.* He wasn't! We were working together for a few weeks. Then I was packing up my van and driving south. The end. Even if the idea of living in the van indefinitely had started to make my heart sink like a ball of lead. It'd been such a freeing adventure at first. But now…

It was a few degrees below freezing, and only a gentle breeze brushed my face. The snow was heavy and full— perfect packing snow. I took a break to chug from my bottle of water while Caleb started another row.

Leaning against the truck's side railing, I watched him surreptitiously. He'd shoved his hat in his pocket like I had. Earlier in the morning it was colder, but exertion had soon dampened my hair under the wool.

Caleb reached the end of the row of fifteen trees— close enough that I could see him clearly but far enough that he didn't realize I was watching. He took off his orange helmet and swiped his arm over his forehead.

Slowly circling his head, he stretched his neck, taking off a glove to scratch his scalp. I could imagine the scrape of his short nails, and a shiver skipped down my spine.

He lifted his arms, clasping one wrist and stretching his back and sides. Left. Right. Arching his spine, then rounding it and stretching forward, arms out.

I took another gulp of cold water. I'd need an icy shower soon if I wasn't careful. Jesus, I was acting like I was back in high school. Time to stop ogling Caleb. I bent to form a snowball in my gloved hands.

It really was perfect snow. Maybe I should roll up a snowman for Ella to bark at suspiciously and topple. Smiling at the thought, I tossed the snowball from hand to hand. The gray sky felt low and heavy, more flakes definitely on the way.

I'd hopped onto the Wi-Fi at the house before we drove out, and the weather report called for the temperature to decline around noon with the wind picking up and drier snow on the way. The kind I'd hated as a kid because it prickled your skin and wasn't good for packing.

Still tossing the ball from hand to hand, I sighed. We'd better get as many trees stacked on the truck as possible before we had to quit for the day. I turned in a circle, peering at the horizon. Still visible, so the storm wasn't rolling in yet.

I jolted as I finished my slow turn to find Caleb about ten feet away, eyebrow cocked and helmet back on. He took out his earplugs and asked, "Should I arm myself?"

It took a few seconds to understand. I found myself grinning as I tossed the snowball high and caught it.

"Only if you want to get your ass kicked."

Wait. No. Why did I say that? We had to cut down a few more rows and get stacking. No time for ogling or playing. I shouldn't want to do either of those activities with Caleb Walker anyway. So why was I still smiling at him and tossing the snowball up and down?

It thwacked my palm with satisfying weight with each catch. Caleb slowly bent to place his chainsaw on the ground. Not making any sudden movements, watching me through his thick lashes. He'd always had such pretty brown eyes.

The snowball he hurled was packed with only a few rapid squeezes, but it still hit my chest with a surprisingly powerful impact. As Caleb dove and rolled for cover behind the next row of thick fir trees still standing, I threw my snowball, striking his leg.

It was on.

All thoughts of work and the fact that I wasn't supposed to be having fun with Caleb abandoned me as I lunged behind the rear of the truck for cover. On my knees, I packed a few more snowballs, squinting around the big tire.

I ducked back as a snowball rocketed toward me. Taking turns advancing and retreating, we hurled missiles and smack-talked, keeping our helmets tugged low. "Is that all you've got?" I yelled as Ella skidded into the line of fire to investigate this new development.

She barked, tail wagging furiously. Caleb called, "Oh, I've got moves you can't even imagine."

Lust tugged tight in my belly. I realized this was the first time he'd sounded relaxed and playful. All week, he'd answered any questions and asked a few, but we'd worked in silence most of the time. He'd been tentative, like he was tiptoeing on eggshells around me.

Now, he laugh-snorted at his own trash talk, and the sound hit me harder than any snowball. Right in the feels, as the kids probably never said anymore.

I'd forgotten that sound.

The unselfconscious, gawky, genuine expression of joy that Caleb only made when he was truly relaxed.

Breathing hard, I hunched behind the tire, completely under the truck now. I remembered the first time I'd heard that snort. We'd been paired randomly by Ms. Singh for the term project in science, and Caleb had barely said a word for the first week of planning.

I'd figured Mr. Captain of the Hockey Team was too good to be friendly with the likes of me. I was just a normal kid—not a geek but not super popular. But that day as we walked to my house after school, I said something prickly and sarcastic about… Shit, I couldn't remember.

Whatever it was, it'd made Caleb laugh. *Really* laugh—that wonderful guffaw coupled with an honest-to-god snort. His cautious, protective layer had been peeled away with that laugh.

We hadn't ended up doing any work on the project when we got to my house, instead stuffing ourselves with microwave popcorn and playing Nintendo. He'd let Sara take turns, and I'd only really minded because I wanted him all to myself.

We'd ordered pizza and played and played until it got so late my mom told Caleb he had to call home so his dad didn't worry and that she'd drive him. I'd gone with them, and on the way back, Mom had simply smiled and said Caleb was cute. I'd been glad it was dark since I was blushing so furiously.

I'd wanted to kiss him that night when he'd had tomato sauce on his face, a lingering splotch at the corner of his mouth… I'd wanted to kiss him so many times after that too.

With a happy squeak, Ella was in my face, licking me frantically. I batted her away. "Okay, okay."

"Are you just going to hide all day?" Caleb called. "Can't take the heat?"

I slithered backwards, gathering my arsenal. "Oh, you want heat?" What was I even saying? All I knew was my heart pounded, and my blood sang with excitement. There was nothing wrong in having a little fun, was there? Even if Caleb had broken my h—

Nope! Enough of that.

I crept around the other side of the truck. Breathing shallowly, I crouched at the ready, now north of the tree where Caleb hid. I didn't move a muscle, listening intently. Aside from Ella's panting as she raced over to Caleb, all was still.

My van might get nippy, but one of the things I did love about winter was the peace of the land muffled in snow. It was—

The snowball whapped me right in the face as I peeked out. Ella was back, tail wagging, having clearly given away my new location. I brushed the cold, wet snow from my face and exclaimed, "Judas dog!"

This earned another snort-laugh from Caleb, and fuck me, I wanted more. I wanted to make him laugh and see his slightly crooked smile. As I hurled a snowball at him, going up on one knee for better control, a voice inside me shouted that I shouldn't want anything from Caleb but to never see him again.

Yet that thought, even after only a week, brought a surge of acid in my gut. It was ludicrous. He was a stranger. It'd been more than a decade! I should be perfectly capable of spending my days with him as a temporary colleague.

Maybe it would be easier if we were in some sea of cubicles passing each other at the water cooler. Instead of grunting and sweating and working our bodies side by side out here with nothing but trees and snow and a naughty beagle.

Where I could hear him snort-laugh and want to tumble him back into the snow and kiss his crooked smile and lick his dimples and—

With a burst of adrenaline, I charged, snowballs cradled in the crook of my left arm as I fired them with my right, dodging Caleb's missile. He yelped, tossing another snowball and scrambling to pack more as I closed in, his helmet falling off.

On his knees, he held up one arm over his face, laughing. "I surrender!"

I had one more snowball in my grasp, my hand raised to fire. "Oh, come on. You're giving up so easily? Coward."

Like a snap of fingers, the mood veered—then crashed and burned. Caleb's smile vanished as he dropped his arm. I stood frozen, my chest heaving. That word—*coward*—seemed to fill the damp air, like the echo of a gong or beat of a drum that matched my thundering pulse.

Lowering his head, Caleb sat back on his heels. Ella nosed at him, tail thrashing, and he petted her. I'd said it without thinking. I hadn't meant it as an attack or to reference the past. But apparently that word hit home with Caleb.

Maybe I should have felt a sense of satisfaction. He'd hurt me so badly when we were young. The voice reminded me that he *should* be sorry. He should feel guilty. He *had* been a coward.

So why did I loathe seeing the defeated slump of his shoulders? Why did I want to make him smile and snort and tell him it was okay? The past was done. We couldn't change it. What was I proving by holding a grudge?

I couldn't seem to say any of it, so I dropped the snowball at my feet. "We should get back to work."

He hopped up, avoiding my gaze. "Yep." He didn't drag his heels at all, getting right to business. Following orders and working hard. I couldn't ask for more.

I couldn't want more. Shouldn't.

Won't. I won't.

We settled back into the rhythm of the job. After an hour, the temperature was plummeting, and blustery gusts of wind were more frequent by the minute. We'd have to pack up soon before the snow squalls whipped in.

I turned in time to see the chainsaw kick back and slam him off his feet, his shout echoing across the snow-muffled forest.

Chapter Four

Caleb

Gasping hoarsely, I blinked at nothing but white snow. It was cold on my face, and the helmet dug into my ear painfully. My right shoulder burned with the force of the chainsaw wrenching it.

I still gripped the saw in both hands. On my side in the snow, I carefully switched it off as strong hands grabbed me, touching arms, back, sides, legs—I was relieved as Blake came into view, examining me. Who else had I expected?

He was talking, but the world was muted. The drum of my heartbeat filled my senses. I blinked up at his gorgeous face over me. His goggles and helmet were gone. I was on my back now, though I couldn't remember rolling over.

I said, "What?"

Mouth tight, Blake bit the end of one glove, yanking

it off. His bare fingers were cold on my ear, and as the pressure released with the earplug and sound rushed back, I finally realized what he was doing.

"Right, earplugs," I mumbled, the fog lifting. I closed my eyes for a second as I arched my back and tested my limbs, which all functioned. "Shit. Guess the chain got pinched. Yanked me with so much force. Wow."

A coarse, wet tongue lapped at my cheek. Jerking, I opened my eyes to find Ella in my face, Blake gently trying to push her away. I laughed. "For a second, I thought it was you licking me."

I guessed I was fine because here I was, back to saying the stupidest things. Blake was practically straddling me, leaning over to remove the other earplug, his fingers sparking heat even though I was sprawled in the snow.

My body wasn't sure whether to rush blood to my sore shoulder or my dick. Why was I such a disaster? "I don't even know how it happened," I said. "The blade pinching. Not you licking my face." Oh, god. "But you weren't."

Ella determinedly squirmed under Blake's arm, shoving her muzzle against my neck as I petted her with my left hand, laughing. "Thanks, girl."

"Did you hit your head?" Blake demanded.

"No. It was just a shock for a second there. I'm okay." I pushed to sitting, and Blake shifted back on his knees in the snow like I was about to bite. Though he had been practically on top of me—which was *not* something to think about now.

Maybe later, when I was alone in my bed. Even if I'd feel even lonelier after jerking off. I'd tried not to think of him when I touched myself. Failed for years. No signs of change.

"You're sure you didn't hit your head? No injuries?"

"I'm sure." As the shock wore off, my right shoulder protested, but it was still in its socket and could pipe down. I'd take an Advil when I got home. The thought of that dark, cold cottage waiting for me twisted my guts.

Ella nosed at me again, darting back and forth between me and Blake. He huffed out a breath, his face softening as she licked his chin. "Yes, yes," he murmured to her. "I love you too."

Those three words were both everything I wanted to hear and a punch in the junk. "Better get back to it." As I shifted to my knees, my navy work pants wet and cold now, I bit back a gasp at the flare of pain in my shoulder.

Blake narrowed his gaze. "Are you hurt?" He shooed Ella away.

"Nah. It's nothing."

His expression darkened. "Don't lie to me!" he barked, then blinked like he was surprised by his own words. "I just mean—if you're hurt it won't help to cover it up. Accidents happen. Nick and Hunter will understand. They wouldn't hold it against you."

I nodded seriously. "I'm not lying to you. Or them. Or anyone." Not ever again. I rolled my shoulder. "Jammed it a bit. The… What did you call it? That force wrenched my arm and I landed on my shoulder. Not dislocated, so it's been way worse. I popped it in grade ten when Jimmy Laverty checked me into the boards. Remember that?"

Eyes boring into me like he was trying to read my soul, he shook his head. "I didn't know you until grade eleven. That first science project." He looked away and pushed to his feet. "We need to—oh, shit."

I followed his gaze to the horizon, but all I saw was snow from my position. Careful not to wince, I stood and…

All I saw was snow.

"Shit!" I agreed. The western horizon was white, the ridge completely vanished as the storm system descended.

"We've got to load these trees and get the truck back."

Nodding, I followed his lead, stowing our saws and other equipment as snow began to fall. Dry flakes at first—not the big, fluffy flakes for building forts and catching on your tongue. This snow was sharp and dry, like pellets on your face.

Even assuming the long, winding drive to the farm was plowed, I didn't like my chances at visibility. Whatever. I'd worry about that later. Add it to the list.

The hired plow had been along the service road that morning, but as we carefully made our way, Ella fidgeting on my lap and bumping her nose on the window, the landscape became whiter and whiter.

Hands tight on the wheel, Blake leaned forward

intently. "I dunno," he muttered. "This is getting dicey."

"Yeah." I squeezed the door handle to my right, ignoring the ache in my shoulder. I kept my left arm hooked protectively around Ella. "Maybe it'll blow through fast."

He geared down, the truck's engine rumbling. We crept along, the service road barely visible, everything white. If the road curved even a bit, we could end up off it in a blink. I tried to remember the road's path. I was sure it did rise and fall and curve with the landscape in places.

Blake cursed under his breath. "Knew this storm was coming. Shouldn't have been fooling around having snowball fights."

"Sorry."

He blew out a breath. "Not your fault. I'm in charge, remember?"

My belly tightened, my mouth going dry. "Yeah. I have to do what you tell me."

I swear to god, the air in the truck's cab might as well have lit on fire. It was freezing outside—the wind howling, snow blowing—but my whole body went hot. I hadn't meant it to sound like…like *that*. I could barely breathe, and Blake seemed like a statue beside me.

Or maybe he was only concentrating on the disappearing road? Maybe I was imagining this electric tension. Maybe he wasn't thinking about telling me to do anything except my job. This job I wanted so much. Needed.

If only I didn't need him. Want him.

Be brave.

No. I couldn't cross that line.

The truck crawled until Blake slammed on the brakes, almost shouting, "There!" He pointed to the left.

Squinting, I could make out a light. "The house? Are we back?"

"I wish. That's Herman. I left on the flood lights attached to the roof just in case. He'll have to do while we wait. It's still three clicks to the house. I don't think it's safe to drive. This whiteout is too dense."

"Wait in your van? Both of us?"

Reaching out to pat Ella, he smiled swiftly, his eyes not meeting mine. "The three of us. Her nose would get her anywhere she wants to go but we're not taking chances."

He leaned across and opened the glove box, pulling out her leash. His arm brushed my knee. I shivered and held my breath until he was climbing out of the cab.

With our woolen hats on and hoods up, and Ella tugging on the leash I had twisted around my left fist, we hiked through grids of trees toward that light. It flickered in and out of sight. At least with the grids we knew where we were walking and that the ground was clear between the neat rows of trees.

Some only came to my waist, while others were over my head and ready to be harvested. Shouting over the wind, I asked, "Doesn't a flood light drain the battery?"

"It can, but I don't use it much. It's got a setting to

automatically activate when it's dim enough, so it wouldn't have switched on until the snow squalls blew in." He held up a gloved hand in front of his face. "Jesus, this wind."

Heads down, we trudged on, Ella tugging and yipping. The floodlight got brighter and brighter. The driving snow battered my face. My nose and lips were so cold they practically burned. Good thing Blake and I had facial hair.

Just getting to the van took so much focus that it wasn't until I stood inside that it hit me. I'd be seeing Blake's bedroom. His whole home. Right here. I wiped snow from my beard and sat on the van's passenger seat, which was turned to face the back. Blake closed the sliding door, and the relief from the biting wind was immediate even if the van was cold.

There was a mat in front of the side sliding door we'd entered through, and I quickly took off my boots before snow got all over the wood floor. I was surprised to see wood in a van, but this was like a small RV. I yanked off my gloves and ran my thawing fingertips over the planks.

"It's that super durable laminate that looks like wood," Blake said, kneeling by Ella and brushing snow from her fur as her tail wagged hard.

"Nice. I'll have to look into it. The floors at the cottage are ancient. The wood's rotting in the corners."

Tossing his hat into a narrow bin between the front seats, Blake looked at me. "That place on Lake Olsen?

You still have it?"

"Uh-huh. I'm living there now."

He made a little listening sound as he unzipped his coat. He wasn't looking at me now. "I guess it's just you out there? Like you said."

He seemed…intense all of a sudden. Like he was pretending not to be interested but actually was very, very interested. My stomach swooped as I said, "Uh-huh."

"Peaceful." Blake shifted and banged his elbow. "Roomier than Herman." He grimaced.

"Only just, but yeah. This is nice, though. You said it wasn't ultra-luxury but it's pretty fancy. This is a supersized van."

"You wouldn't believe how some people have fixed up their vans, but yeah. Thanks." Blake seemed to relax as he tugged on a curtain behind the driver's seat. Both front seats were captain's chairs. "Can close this if I want. And obviously this is the fridge and sink."

Below a window on the driver's side, a mini fridge with a butcher block counter sat, the sink to the left. There were clever shelves and a dish rack that folded down over the sink for drying. Every space seemed to be utilized.

Behind the sliding door on the left was a small table and chair bolted to the floor. Beyond the kitchen, a pocket door slid open to reveal a narrow toilet stall on the side of the van.

Blake motioned to it and said, "It's a tight squeeze

with the door shut, but doable."

"It's great!" I gave him a smile. "Honestly, this is so smart. You've got so much stuff in here." I peered at the rear of the van as I scratched behind Ella's ears. A double mattress filled the space, neatly made with a thick duvet in forest green. "I like your bed."

As soon as the words left my mouth, I flushed with heat. I shouldn't be talking about Blake's bed. Or should I? Was it weird? Or was it weird *not* to? My pulse raced. "Not that I—" Nope. Making it worse. Shut up.

Blake laughed thinly. "Thanks. It's a quality mattress. Nice and firm. I can open the back doors in good weather. It's a nice way to wake up." He motioned at the rear of the van. Blinds made of woven fibers covered the back windows, and he leaned over to pull them up, squinting and grimacing.

The blinds on the van's other windows were lifted, and I peered out too. Nothing but white. We were cut off from the world, which shouldn't have made me so…happy? Excited?

I focused. "Right. Cool." As Ella licked my hand, I glanced around. "Really cool. How do you shower?" Great, now I was asking about him being naked.

Blake grimaced. "That's probably the biggest flaw with this van. In warm weather, I've got a solar shower bag on the roof attached to a hose. The sun heats the water and then gravity makes it a shower through the hose and nozzle."

"Oh, wow. Great idea."

"Too bad it's not viable in the winter. One of the reasons I head south after the holidays. I can deal with washing my hair in the sink and sponge bathing for a month or so but that's it."

Oh, wow. Wow. Wooooow. The thought of Blake naked and washing himself with a cloth, or maybe an actual sponge… Or what were those things from the ocean? A loofah? The thought of him naked and dragging something wet over his bare body—

I almost shouted, "Pipes don't freeze?"

"Not yet. My dad made sure to insulate them really well so they don't burst."

I nodded. "Maybe he can help me in the cottage. I need to hire a plumber, but I can't afford it yet. So far, so good, but once we get into the deep freeze, I dunno. It's an old setup. I might wake up with no water one morning."

Blake frowned. "I might be able to help. My dad's buddy Rich is a plumber. Bet I could call in a favor."

"Yeah? That would be awesome." Warmth flushed my chest. The idea that Blake would want to help me at all made me stupidly happy.

"Sure." He knelt and opened the fridge, his denim-clad ass right there. I wouldn't even have to stretch to touch it…

Occupying my hands petting Ella, I looked out the sliding door's window. "Man. Nothing but white."

"Good thing we can wait it out. Hunter and Nick were smart to go to the city earlier. You hungry?"

"Always. My dad used to say I had a hollow leg."

Blake chuckled. "I remember that."

The van was warming up, but I rubbed my hands together before petting Ella again as she whined. The whining continued while Blake made sandwiches with cold cuts, the van just tall enough for him to stand at the sink.

"I guess you can have some people food, girl," Blake said. "I know you love carrots and those are allowed."

I asked, "So there's no signal at all to text Hunter and Nick? You don't need the internet for your writing?"

He shook his head as he pushed up the sleeves of his blue sweater. Blake's forearms were sprinkled with light brown hair. I watched as he spread mayo on slices of bread, the muscles flexing slightly as he moved.

He said, "No. Have to go to the house to connect to the Wi-Fi. They have an old landline too for emergencies." He ducked his head to peer out the window, wiping condensation with his palm. "Can't walk to the house until the snow squalls pass. Too easy to get turned around with no visibility." He laughed sharply. "As for writing, not being able to waste hours online is supposed to be helping me concentrate. Allegedly."

I smiled and nodded to the small table and upholstered chair. "Is that where you write?"

"Allegedly." He opened a drawer and pulled out two melamine plates with pineapples on them. "You still like pickles?"

"Yeah. Thanks." He remembered I liked pickles. It

made my chest tight with excitement instead of the usual stress.

Blake put a handful of ketchup chips onto each plate. I asked, "Still your favorite?"

"Yep." He popped a chip into his mouth and then sucked red powder from his index finger.

One plate in his other hand, he turned from the small counter—finger still in his mouth. He froze, and we stared at each other in the small space. Then he yanked his finger free with a soft, wet *pop.*

My dick swelled in my work pants. I wanted him to suck me. I wanted him to suck me the way he had our first and only time together. I had half a mind to drop from the low chair right onto my knees and beg.

Ella's yip broke the spell, and Blake practically slammed the plate on the little table, a few chips sliding off. They barely even landed before Ella snapped them up. We laughed, and my heart hammered.

"Maybe I should hire her for cleaning," Blake joked. "Do you want to sit here?"

"Nah. I'm good." If I stood, my hard-on would be incredibly obvious. I accepted the other plate, and Blake took the chair at the table facing me after dropping a few baby carrots on the floor for Ella.

I really was hungry. I moaned, swallowing a bite of the sandwich. "Hits the spot. Thanks again."

"Sure. No prob." Blake kept his eyes on his plate.

It wasn't possible that he wanted me too, was it? I guess it was *possible*, but incredibly unlikely. He was only being nice. We were stuck here in close quarters. He was being a good host.

I ate the dill pickle he'd fished out of a jar from the fridge. "Are your books in space?"

His gaze met mine as he swallowed a bite. I watched his throat work. "My books?"

"Yeah. Are they sci-fi? You always loved that stuff. Like those books. *The Expanse*?"

"You remember that?" He cleared his throat. "Want a beer? Safe to say we're done work for the day."

"I should probably stick to water or coffee. Or pop if you have any. The roads will be a mess."

Blake's brow furrowed, and he squinted out the window beside him before checking his watch. "Getting dark soon with these short December days. Maybe you should stay over at the house. We can walk there once we can see. Don't think it's a good idea to drive anywhere."

I really could have used a drink for my bone-dry throat. The idea of sleeping under the same roof with Blake sent my head spinning.

"There are a couple of guest rooms, I think," Blake added quickly. "I'm pretty sure."

"Right." I nodded. "Beer. Sure. Please can I have one, I mean."

He jumped up and opened the fridge—his ass practically in my face this time. Ella had finished her carrots, and she squeezed between the door and his calf, her tail wagging hard. Blake laughed. "You can have more carrots. That's it."

He removed the cap and passed me a bottle of Moosehead, and I almost dropped it as our fingers brushed. "Slippery," I muttered before gulping.

"Bet you're thirsty too, huh?" Blake murmured to Ella. He filled a yellow bowl with water for her and placed it at the foot of the sink unit. He sat and sipped his own beer.

We finished eating. We drank our beer. It was awkward and weird, and I desperately wanted to say something smart or funny or cute. Something Blake would like. Something that would make Blake like *me*.

Be brave.

I finished my Moosehead. "So, what *are* your books about?"

He shrugged, fidgeting. "Space, like you said. Adventure stuff. It's not literature or anything."

I smiled. "I don't know who you think you're talking to, but I'm not exactly big on *literature*."

Blake huffed out a laugh, but his brow furrowed as if he thought it was a good question: Who *was* he talking to? Or maybe I was reading too much into it. I asked, "Do you write them under another name? I couldn't find them."

His eyebrows shot up. "You looked?"

I almost laughed it off and said I was only curious. But hadn't I promised myself no more lies? "Yeah. I'd love to read them."

"Really?" Blake spun his empty beer bottle between his hands. "Okay. My pen name's Cassian Kinsman.

64

'Blake Martin' sounded too ordinary for space adventures."

"I like it." I pulled my phone from my pocket before remembering there was no signal. "Do you have paperbacks?" I wanted to see his work. Hold it in my hands. He'd always had a great imagination. It made total sense to me that he'd become a writer.

"Yeah, but I don't have any here." Sitting sideways, he crossed his legs, and his foot jiggled. He wore beige moccasins that looked fuzzy and warm and were probably a gift from his mom. He said, "Every inch counts." A blush rose behind his light beard. "Of space. Space is at a premium when you live in a van."

"Got it." I ordered myself not to think about anything else measured in inches or centimeters or any other unit. Also no thinking about units. "So the books do well? Writing's your full-time job?"

"Yep." He smiled for real this time, a pleased little twist of his full lips. "I self-publish the series, and it's done really well. Agents and publishers just take all your money. I've always read sci-fi adventures, and I love writing them. It's built into a steady income. Still, it's great to pick up work here at the farm. I love being outdoors. It's a nice break from hunching over the keyboard."

"That's amazing! Congratulations. You used to tell me the best stories. You remember that? When we'd go out to the pond on Friday nights? Or hang in my room and—"

Most of the time we'd talked and done nothing much. Until that one night a few weeks before graduation. My throat was dry again. I croaked, "Can you tell me what they're about?"

He popped up and refilled Ella's bowl, not looking at me. "Just space adventures."

"Right. Cool. You said."

"Yup." He opened and closed the fridge, getting Ella's undivided attention.

I looked over my right shoulder to check on the snow situation through the windshield, and pain shot through to my neck. I couldn't bite back a wince. In the rapidly falling night, all I could see was snow.

"You said you weren't hurt."

I eased back around to find Blake looming over me. "It's okay. Just have to be a bit careful. I barely noticed it until now." It was the truth. Who had time to concentrate on sore muscles when the man I wanted more than anything was in his fuzzy slippers a few inches away?

"Mmm. I have some Icy Hot. Take off your shirt."

With shaking hands, all I could do was obey. Whether it was brave or foolish, I had no damn clue.

Chapter Five

Blake

*N*OTHING SEXUAL ABOUT *this. Nothing romantic. It's first aid.*

Maybe if I repeated this mantra a few more dozen times I'd believe it.

"Are you sure?" Caleb asked as I rooted around in the box of bathroom and health supplies that lived under the sink. He added, "I probably stink something fierce."

"You want to wash up?" How were these words escaping my mouth? How was this improving the situation? Didn't matter now—I was pulling out the plastic wash basin and filling it with warm water. "The water heater's battery-powered. Does a decent job, but I can always use the kettle if you want it hotter." I squirted about half a bottle of body wash into the basin.

"I'm sure that's fine."

I turned from the sink, soapy water splashing over

the side of the bowl in my hands. Ella barked and sniffed at it, surely wondering what new game this was. Meanwhile, I stood there like a statue watching Caleb unbutton his green flannel work shirt.

His eyes met mine. He was still sitting in the turned passenger seat. Then he stood, the flannel gaping open to reveal a white undershirt. There was barely a foot between us. I'd have to start breathing again once I processed his deliciously hairy chest through the thin cotton.

As Caleb eased the shirt over his shoulder, he bit his lip in obvious pain. Ella whined softly at his feet, head cocked. I practically dropped the basin on the small table, more soapy water sloshing and Ella barking suspiciously as if it hadn't just happened less than a minute ago.

"Here," I said, edging behind him and reaching for the collar of his shirt. The flannel was soft and worn.

Caleb held his arms back a little, making it easier to gently peel the fabric down. He was so *pliable*. I swayed forward, inches from the hair at the back of his neck and the bump at the top of his spine that I could easily lick with just a small movement…

No. Licking. Allowed.

Even if, as I inhaled, his scent filled my nose and triggered sense memory that made my knees weak.

"Sorry," he rasped. "Like I said, I stink."

Jesus, I wanted to bury my face in his armpit. This close to him, memories flooded back—the taste of his mouth and his cock and his jizz leaking from my lips. His hockey jersey crushed under us as we rutted desperately.

I wanted his sweat and his cum and his kisses. Maybe more. Maybe I wanted everything from Caleb Walker.

"Blake?" He started to turn his head.

"Careful," I murmured, stilling him with a simple touch. "Can you raise your left arm?"

Again, he did as I told him, pliable as I maneuvered his tank top off, jostling that right shoulder as little as possible.

"It's really not that bad," he croaked. "But thanks."

I realized I should have left the basin at the sink, so I placed it back there and handed him a clean washcloth because it would have been far too over the top for me to sponge bath him like I was the nurse in some injury fantasy. I sat at the table and busied myself with petting Ella.

Darkness had fully descended outside the cocoon of the van, and Caleb was reflected in the glass of the kitchen window. Not that I was looking. Not at the broad expanse of his bare back or the reflection of his chest. Dark nipples poked out from the generous dusting of brown hair, and I wondered just how red I could make them with my teeth…

Resolutely, I scratched Ella's head, murmuring to her as she gazed up at me with pure affection and adoration. "Good girl," I murmured. "You're so good, aren't you?"

Caleb inhaled raggedly, and I glanced over and

asked, "Okay?" My breath was shallow.

"Mm-hmm!" In the reflection, his head was down as he twisted the cloth in the basin.

Ella bumped my hand with her nose, and I chuckled. "Forgive me, madam."

Keeping my eyes firmly on Ella, I lavished her with attention while trying to ignore the sounds that seemed to be amplified in Herman's close quarters. The van had never seemed quite this small as I listened to the rasp of the cloth over Caleb's skin. The gentle slosh of water in the basin. His faint inhalations and exhalations.

I imagined drawing my fingers over his skin. My lips. My tongue. My teeth. Would Caleb be loud? Or shy and embarrassed the way he'd been years ago? He'd been with other men now—a thought that sent ridiculous jealousy rocketing through me.

"I'm ready."

I jerked my head up to find Caleb facing me. Close enough to touch if I reached out. Close enough to spot the droplets of water suspended in the hair swirling over his chest.

"You have the Icy Hot?" His brows met as he nodded to the tube on the table. He held out his hand for it.

"Right! Yep." I'd unscrewed the lid, and now I grasped the tube so vigorously the gel shot out, a dollop plopping onto the floor and the rest sliding down to coat my fingers. *Smooth.*

Caleb dropped to his knees in a flash, tugging on Ella's collar. "Don't eat that, Ella. Dogs aren't covered by

OHIP."

A laugh rumbled through my chest, warm and oh, so sweet, and Caleb's dimples appeared. I said to Ella, "No, dogs aren't covered by Ontario's health insurance. You're not landing Hunter and Nick a massive vet bill for Icy Hot poisoning on our watch."

Our. A simple three-letter word didn't have the right to make my heart swell.

Caleb had managed to swipe up the spilled gel from the floor, and he spread it over his shoulder. Before I knew what I was doing, I reached out, my goopy fingers meeting his collar bone.

"No sense in it going to waste," I whispered. Why was I whispering?

His brown eyes locked on me, Caleb gave a tiny nod. His lips parted, and he tipped his head to the side. I smoothed my fingers over the long expanse of his neck, gently rubbing the gel into his skin.

He sat back on his heels, his eyes flickering shut as I squeezed more gel from the tube into my palm and spread it over his whole shoulder, dipping over his back, strong muscles flexing beneath my touch. Then back to his neck. Throat. Collarbone.

When my fingertip brushed his nipple, he gasped softly, his eyes flying open. I froze, my lungs burning, my cock painfully hard against my fly. Neither of us moved a muscle until he sucked in a breath, the choppy movement of his chest touching my hovering finger.

Ella whined at the door, and we both jumped, Caleb

pushing to his feet. I exclaimed, "She needs to pee!" and practically lunged for the door. A gust of icy air burst in as I slid it open, and Ella flew out as I lunged for her collar and missed.

"Shit! Ella!" I called, "Don't go far!" and closed the door with a solid thud. "As if she speaks English beyond a few words. I should have put on her leash."

"I'm sure she'll be fine. Beagles have great noses, right?"

"Yeah, and she knows this farm like the back of her hand. Paw."

Caleb peered through the window. "Looks like it stopped snowing anyway." The wind was still blustery, snow flying, so it was hard to tell. "Maybe I should get going."

I didn't want him to go. "You don't know the way to the house on your own." I pressed my face to the glass. "Visibility's still bad." I shifted uncomfortably. "I shouldn't have—sorry. Do you want to borrow a clean shirt? Probably be too tight, but…"

"I'm not sorry."

I had to look at him. We stood facing each other, and I watched him lick his lips before adding, "I mean, I *am* sorry. Not about—" He motioned to his chest, a blush rising up to his neck. Jesus, I wanted to kiss that fevered skin… He took a deep breath. "I want to talk about it. I want to apologize."

We'd skirted the elephant in the room long enough. I nodded, my desire cooling as the old hurt stampeded back.

"When I told you I'd break up with Mel, I meant it. But I should have known it was too scary. Not just breaking up with her—coming out. I wanted to, but I wasn't ready. I was afraid of disappointing Dad. I was afraid he wouldn't want me if I told him the truth. I'm sorry I told you one thing and then didn't do it."

I waited for him to say more, but he only watched me warily. Hopefully? I shook my head. "Wait. You think that's why I was upset? Because you changed your mind?"

"I… Yes?"

Frustration surged like a lit fuse. I clenched my fists, unable to choke down the pain that had festered for years despite my attempts to keep it in the past. "It's because you ghosted me!" Hell. This was a bad idea. This was the last thing I wanted to talk about.

But I was a damn liar, because as Caleb stared at me with wide eyes, more words competed to trip off my tongue, elbowing each other aside.

"If you'd just *told* me. But you never said a word. Not even a text. An emoji. Something. *Anything.*" I cringed at the plaintive tone. I was supposed to be angry, not woeful.

Scratch that. I was supposed to be *over this*. I'd moved on years ago. Caleb wasn't allowed to parachute back into my life and dredge up these raw emotions. These emotions had been cooked. Done, finished, over. Stick a fork in them.

Yet I was still talking.

"You promised me you'd break up with Melissa. It was easy to say after I sucked your cock. I get it. In the cold light of morning, it wasn't so simple."

Caleb's mouth tightened, his shoulders hunching. "I was scared. I didn't want to hurt her." His voice was barely a whisper, but he looked me straight in the eyes. "Or you. But I was a coward. I hurt you both."

"Honestly, it wasn't much of a shock that you were holding hands with Melissa in homeroom the next morning. It…" I inhaled and exhaled deeply. "Yeah, it hurt. I was disappointed. But it—" I broke off as my voice cracked.

"Blake," he whispered. "I'm sorry."

I blinked back tears. "It *killed* me that you wouldn't even look my way. I was invisible. I sent a hundred texts and nothing. *Nothing.* Not even a 'leave me alone' or 'it was a mistake' or 'I'm straight after all, never mind.' Nothing. We were friends." My voice broke again on the last word, and I cringed. "You were the first guy I had the guts to kiss, and you treated me like I was *nothing.*"

"I'm sorry." Caleb's voice grew stronger. "It was wrong. I knew it. I hated it. I hated myself. But I did it anyway. It was like… Like watching from outside my body."

"I finished our science project and put your name on it, and you never even said thank you!" What a weird thing to still care about. Why did I still care about that damn project? "It had been so much fun working on that together. Getting to know you. Realizing that you were more than a jock. Feeling—falling—"

Falling in love.

Forget memory lane—I was careening into the junk-yard where I'd buried my hurt and affection and longing. Wait, why was it a junkyard? You didn't bury things in a junkyard.

While I was worrying about metaphors, Caleb had suddenly closed the distance between us. Which meant taking two strides across the van.

While I was worrying about metaphors, Caleb had dropped to his knees.

"I'm sorry. Please. Please." He stared up at me, those brown eyes beseeching, his hands fidgeting, fingers twitching as if he wanted to reach out but was afraid. As if he wanted to touch me.

He was literally on his knees. Begging. My heart thundered, my chest so tight I could barely breathe. Was this what I wanted? Was it what I needed? And what exactly was "it"? To punish Caleb? Forgive him?

Love him again?

The idea sucker-punched me. Had I ever really stopped loving him—or just told myself I had? Just stopped thinking about it, burying it deep in that junkyard at the end of memory lane or whatever convoluted metaphor I wanted to come up with.

Still on his knees, Caleb dropped his head. "Please."

His hair was thick and smooth under my fingers. Messy and damp at his temple from where he'd washed his face. He froze as I touched him, not seeming to breathe. I brushed back his hair, my whole hand coming to rest on his head.

With a shuddering exhalation, he leaned into my palm, lifting his face, his eyes wide and hopeful.

I barely registered the *crack* as my knees hit the fake wood laminate. I was too busy kissing Caleb Walker again. Tasting him—devouring him—our beards rubbing like two sticks creating sparks, our tongues meeting.

He moaned into my mouth, his thick arms circling me like iron. My hands tangled in his hair, tilting his head to deepen the kiss. He tasted faintly like pickles, and I couldn't get enough of his little gasps and wet lips.

I managed to throw a hand out to break our fall as I toppled him onto his back for more. Needed more. More contact. More friction. More *everything*. I was painfully hard in my jeans, groaning as I rutted against his answering bulge.

I wanted skin to skin, wanted flesh, but I couldn't stop kissing him long enough to rip off my plaid shirt. We couldn't stop humping each other like we were possessed, grunting and gasping, Caleb tugging on my denim-clad ass and grinding.

Grunting. Gasping. Grinding. Nice alliteration there.

I laughed at the bizarre thoughts roaming around my head, kissing Caleb through my wild, frantic smile. Panting, he broke free, blinking up at me in a daze, a bewildered, beautiful smile brightening his face.

Bewildered. Beautiful. Brightening.

Still laughing, I dipped my head and sucked his nipple, grazing it with my teeth, loving the rasp of hair against my face and the arch of Caleb's back as he begged for more.

Begged for *me.*

It took a few seconds to realize my mouth was tingling from traces of Icy Hot, and I would have laughed, but my balls were too tight. I was too close. "*Caleb,*" I moaned.

Thrusting against him, I came, shocked and shaking in his arms. In my jeans like we were back in high school. He gripped my ass tighter, rocking with helpless, eager gasps, his eyes wide and mouth open as he shouted his release.

"Jesus," I mumbled, my mouth at his throat as I relaxed on top of him. I was probably heavy, but he held me close.

"Imagined this for so long." He snort-laughed. "Maybe not exactly like this."

I had to kiss him. "Guess we were channeling those teenage vibes." A fresh wave of desire washed over me. "I'm looking forward to hearing about what you *have* been imagining."

He blushed a darker red under his beard, and I had to kiss him again. As we shifted, he jerked with a wince. I pushed myself up, straddling him.

"Shit! Your shoulder."

"It really is fine." He ran his hands up my chest,

skimming over the buttons of my shirt and fumbling with them. "A little sore, but it's nothing. I just wanted you to play nurse."

"Ah, the truth comes out!" My smile faded as I traced his spit-slick lips with my finger.

Spit-slick lips. Almost rhymes.

"Blake?" he murmured against my fingers, his hands dipping inside my shirt, his palms cool on my chest before warming quickly.

"Guess the truth's out now. And so are you. And we're…"

"Good?"

I nodded. "We're good." Maybe we could be so much more, but for tonight, it was enough. "Apology accepted." Whew. That felt right. I didn't know what tomorrow would bring, but I didn't care.

Tonight was just beginning.

Chapter Six

Caleb

I KISSED BLAKE'S fingers before sucking one into my mouth. He groaned. "Oh yeah, we're good."

Music to my ears. My heart soared, and my head felt woozy in the best way as Blake kissed me. His finger was still hooked into my mouth, his tongue slipping in beside it like he just couldn't wait. Like he wanted to swallow me whole.

He'd taken the lead the first time, but we'd been fumbling and all elbows and awkwardness. Considering we'd come in our pants just now, I probably shouldn't have been patting myself on the back for how experienced we were now.

Especially since I wasn't an expert or anything. Like he read my mind, Blake asked against my mouth. "What are you into?"

I mumbled around his finger, "Anything."

Laughing, he withdrew his finger and traced down my chest with the wet tip. "Want to narrow that down?" Shivers rippled over my skin, my nipples tight.

"Anything," I repeated.

His brow furrowed, and he dragged his blunt nails over my pecs. "You been hooking up lately?"

"A few times. I went to the club in Barrie. There aren't too many guys on the apps around Pinevale."

"Yeah. Most of them are on the down low and married to women. Not my scene."

"Me either." I'd learned my lesson after cheating on Mel with him. It had made me feel like garbage even though I'd loved him.

I still loved him.

I loved making him laugh when I wasn't even trying. I wanted to make him laugh again, but he was straddling my waist, and all I could concentrate on was touching his thighs and wishing we were naked.

"So, what are you into these days?" he asked.

"Dunno."

"You must have some idea. Top? Bottom? Both? Neither? Voyeurism?" He grinned. "Clearly we both enjoy frotting."

I smiled too. "Yeah. Isn't, like, porn voyeurism? Watching?"

"Mmm. What do you like watching?"

I needed another beer. "I'm not picky."

"But when you're scrolling through thumbnails with names like 'Dominant Cocky Jock' and 'Straight Guy

Barebacked by Roommate' or 'Twink Sucks Doctor,' which ones do you click on?"

My face flushed hot as I laughed. "Do you still have a scary good memory, or did you make those up?"

He grinned. "Both." Leaning over me, he nipped my earlobe before sucking it slowly. His breath was warm on my ear. "Tell me what you want. Tell me what you like."

My throat was a desert. "I like watching guys get…"

"Fucked? Pounded by Daddy? Buggered ten ways to Sunday? Destroyed by massive cocks? Bent over and—"

"Yes, yes! All of those." We were both laughing, and I covered my face with my hand. I hadn't spent much time talking with the guys I'd messed around with. I opened my eyes as Blake eased my hand away.

He smiled down softly. "Have you tried it? Bottoming? That's what you want?"

I nodded. "A few times. One of them seemed surprised I wanted that. I guess I don't look the part."

Blake rolled his eyes. "Small minds. How was it?"

"Okay. Most of the time they wanted me to fuck them."

"And you're not into it?"

"Sometimes."

"What do you think about most when you're turned on?" He traced my nipple with his finger. "When you need to get off." He dragged his finger across my chest to my other nipple, which hardened before he even touched it. "When you're so wound up it hurts, and you need to get there fast and furious. What do you think about?"

Words were not happening. I was hard again, and I squirmed under Blake, needing pressure on my cock—which was trapped in my sticky underwear. I guess the *ugh* showed on my face since Blake frowned.

I said, "Can we get out of these pants?"

"Now that you mention it, let's." He pushed to his feet, and I was cold on the floor without his body heat. He reached down a hand for me, pulling me up. I winced at the stiffness in my knee. Blake asked, "Your shoulder?"

"Knee this time. It's healed, but it's never been the same."

"A shame, especially with how much you want to be on your knees."

"No, no, it's fine! I can still—" I cleared my throat. "You know."

Blake laughed softly. "Oh, don't worry." He kissed me long and slow and dirty, his tongue curling around mine. He whispered, "I know. I know what you need." He stepped away suddenly, and I swayed after him as he said, "First things first."

We stripped off, and I watched as Blake filled the basin with more warm water and a squirt of soap. I still had my socks on, but Blake was totally naked except for his moccasins. Damn, his ass was amazing. His body was long and lean and strong, light brown hair dusting his skin. I leaned to my left to get a better peek at his junk.

Giving me a sly smile, he dipped the cloth in the basin and squeezed before slowly turning to face me. He ran the cloth under his arms, then slowly across his belly. I could see the jizz crusted in his pubes, which were darker. He rinsed the cloth, then scooped up suds and slowly, *slowly* washed his hard cock and heavy balls clean.

The only sounds were the drag of the cloth and my panting. I was so hard, and I didn't care if I was sticky. "Can I?—I need—now. Please."

He stroked his thick, juicy shaft with the cloth, pretending to be all casual about it. "Hmm? What do you need?"

"To suck you."

His Adam's apple bobbed. "Should I let you?"

I nodded. "I have to do what you say. You're in charge."

"*Jesus*," he mumbled, tossing the cloth behind him without looking before striding the few steps to me and pushing me to sit on the side of the bed. "Go on. Suck me."

I ducked my head and swallowed him, almost choking. I drew back enough to breathe around his throbbing cock before I sucked for all I was worth. He tangled his hands in my hair, and I bobbed my head, inhaling his musk.

"Fuck, yes," he muttered. "Caleb."

I groaned around his cock, my lips stretching, spit leaking down my chin.

"Caleb," he repeated, and I groaned again. The sound of my name while he filled me, rocking into me with little thrusts now, was like Christmas morning.

"You like it when I fuck your mouth?" he murmured.

I nodded as best I could, his pubes tickling my nose, a stray soap bubble popping with the smell of orange.

"Lie back." This was a command, louder and powerful.

I obeyed, the top of my head brushing the rear van doors as I lay back sideways across the bed, my feet still on the floor, my socks sliding. Blake crawled over me, his balls swinging in my face.

Opening my mouth, I sucked and licked his balls as he moaned. Damn, it was so good to hear that sound from him, knowing it was because of me. That I was giving him pleasure. If I'd reached down and tugged my dick, I would have come again already.

I didn't. I wasn't ready to come yet. I ran my hands up and down Blake's bare thighs, his muscles flexing as I sucked his balls. I glimpsed the shiny head of his cock as he shifted down, and I opened wide for him.

"Going to fuck your mouth now," he muttered, shoving between my lips.

I breathed hard through my nose as he rocked. It was suffocating, my nose in his belly, my jaw open as wide as I could get it. I tasted salty pre-cum and swallowed around his shaft as he gasped.

Then he was gone, a cool wash of air on my hot face. I whimpered, reaching for him as he returned to the sink.

He laughed shakily. "Not yet. As much as I'd love to shoot down your throat, there's something else I want more."

"Do we have to pick?"

His laugh was deeper now, his eyes crinkling. "No, but I'm not ready to come yet."

"Right. Okay." I'd just been thinking the same thing, after all.

Blake's smile became a smirk. Wet cloth in hand, he licked his lips. "Turn over. Hands and knees."

My heart hammered so loudly I could have been wearing earplugs. I shifted onto all fours, my ass now on display. I looked out the van's back windows, but I could only see my own reflection. My hair stuck up, my mouth hung open, my chest heaving.

Blake behind me. He didn't notice me watching in the window, his eyes locked on my ass as he smoothed his palm over my hip and asked, "This okay for your shoulder?" I nodded. It still tingled with the Icy Hot. "Your knee?" I nodded again.

He stripped off my socks. I waited, my breath fogging the window.

"You're so fucking hot, you know that?" Blake said, running a hand up and down my quivering side. He dipped under me, picking up the cloth and roughly cleaning my groin as I gasped and bit my lip. Warm water ran down my inner thighs.

Then he drew the cloth back between my legs, spreading my ass open. The wet, textured cloth rubbed my hole and up my whole crack, then back down and up again. I collapsed to my elbows, totally exposed.

"*Blake.*"

His breath brushed my hole as he nudged my knees wider. I didn't care about the sore tug in my neck as I craned back to see him fall to his knees beside the bed. His beard scraped my tender skin as he—*god*—buried his face in my ass.

He licked my hole, his tongue fucking into me as I made noises I didn't know were possible. My dick *ached*, my balls so full, pleasure radiating. I was going to come just from Blake's tongue in my ass, and I cried out.

The sharp noise just outside made us both jump, and I banged the top of my head on the rear door. "Ow!"

Blake's hands tightened on my hips as his laughter brushed over my ass with a warm puff. "Ella's worried about you." He drew me back, shifting us so we were both on the bed the right way, the van wide enough that I could stretch out on the mattress fully, my head on the pillows. He kicked off his moccasins.

I called hoarsely, "Everything's fine, girl, thank you!" She barked again, and we laughed.

Blake kissed the top of my head. "Okay?"

"Uh-huh. You can go back to that."

He pressed me down, his weight over my back and legs. "Can I? I'm supposed to be in charge here." He licked down my spine, and I humped the mattress, desperate for pressure.

"Please," I begged.

"Mmm." Blake dipped his fingers into my crease. "Have to fuck you now. Is that what you want?"

"Yes." I'd never had it like this. Never begged anyone. Never trusted anyone enough to plead for their cock in me. Even though I'd come out, I'd never let anyone see me this bare and needy. This real.

My throat was suddenly painfully thick, tears burning my eyes. I was alone and scared, running out of money with no idea what my life was going to be. Or…I had been. Because now I wasn't alone. I was with the man I'd never stopped loving all these years.

The sob burst through my clenched jaw, and the next thing I knew Blake was rolling me onto my back and peering down at me with worry. Tears leaked from my eyes even as I tried to smile. "S'okay," I mumbled.

He brushed back my hair. "What is it?"

"I'm not lonely anymore." I realized as soon as I said it that it was too much pressure to put on him. I'd apologized, and he'd accepted, and now we were fucking, but I shouldn't get ahead of myself. "I mean—you don't have to. I'm just happy. But I know we're not…"

Blake's face creased as he put a finger to my lips. "Shh. I'm here. I'm here."

I nodded. I couldn't worry about tomorrow. Tonight, I was in Blake's bed, and it was everything I'd dreamed about. "Please."

There was no smirk or teasing now as he fumbled for lube and a condom. I wasn't very flexible, but I spread my legs and held my thighs up as high as I could as he inched into me. Our chests rose and fell quickly, sweat dampening our skin, or maybe it was the leftover water from the cloth.

I was so full with Blake inside me, stretching me with hard thrusts, and it was only when he slapped his hand over my mouth that I realized Ella was barking again outside and I was moaning and making all kinds of sounds.

He grinned. "I know my cock is magnificent but do try to control yourself." He squeezed a hand between us, jerking my dick in time with a powerful snap of his hips. "But don't. Let go. It's okay. I'm here. I've got you."

I groaned against his palm, squeezing his cock inside me, spread open and filled so completely I could barely stand it even though it was perfect.

"I want you to come, Caleb. You have to do what I tell you, remember?" Blake stroked my cock fast with his slick hand, and I strained into his touch, my balls drawing up, the thick, powerful tension building until it burst.

I shook in Blake's arms, sweet fire burning me alive as I spurted and cried out. He pounded my ass, and I wished he could fill me with his cum as his orgasm took him. Face in my neck, his teeth sharp and lips wet, he moaned my name.

A howl echoed from outside, and all we could do was laugh.

"I'M FINE, I promise!" I turned my head on the pillow,

squirming away from Ella's enthusiastic kisses.

"Kicked out of my own bed. Replaced so easily."

I glared at Blake standing by the little stove. He'd opened the door for Ella and wrapped himself in a thick plaid blanket, moccasins on his feet again. He stirred the small pot of milk, and two packets of powdered hot chocolate waited with alligator mugs from Florida. The alligators were wearing sunglasses.

Ella wriggled closer as I tried to gently push her away. "I'm fine, thank you."

"She's worried I was murdering you. I'm the dastardly sort." He whistled softly. "Ella, what's this?" He'd taken out the bag of baby carrots, and now he dropped a few on the floor. Ella flew off the bed so fast she should have left skid marks.

"Oh, now I'm chopped liver?" I laughed, pulling the duvet back up over my naked body.

"She's a fickle mistress," Blake agreed. He leaned close to the window on the sliding door. "Snow's definitely stopped. We should head out to the house soon. Beagles cannot live by carrots alone."

The cozy afterglow evaporated. "Oh. Right." If the hired plow came soon, there'd be no reason for me to stay. It was fine. I couldn't expect…what? I wasn't sure. What *could* I expect? Had this meant anything to Blake? It had seemed like it.

He stirred the milk with a regular metal spoon that circled the stainless steel pot with a scraping noise that had been weirdly soothing before. Now it set my teeth on edge.

It was *fine*. I'd go home, and I'd see Blake tomorrow. I couldn't rush and expect more. Even if I felt boneless and wrung out. The sex had been amazing. I'd run miles in basic training carrying a loaded pack and hadn't felt this wrecked.

"You okay?" Blake asked. The spoon scraped.

I almost said *fine* or *yeah* or another lie. I didn't want to lie. I mean, I'd *cried* while Blake fucked me. He hadn't run screaming from that, so…

Be brave.

"Caleb?"

"I don't want to go home."

Hot chocolate package in hand, Blake froze. "Tonight? I don't want you to go either."

My breath whooshed out. "You don't?"

"No! We have to go to the house to get Ella dinner and call Hunter and Nick to let them know everything's fine here. I was thinking we'd sleep in the guest room. Together."

I curled onto my side, facing him. "That would be cool. The cottage is… I guess I don't like being out there on my own. It was okay in the summer with lots of people up from the city, but there aren't too many year-rounders."

He nodded. "You could always stay here. Closer to work. Oh, shit!" Blake grabbed the pot by its handle just as milk boiled over in a foamy eruption. He tossed his blanket onto the chair and picked up the kitchen cloth.

My heart thudded. "Until you go south, you mean?"

Blake frowned as he wiped up milk. Some of it dripped to the floor, much to Ella's delight. "Yeah. We can just—we have weeks. Lots of work and the holiday festival on the weekends. Then Christmas. We could just… See how it goes?"

I tried not to get ahead of myself, but the thought of staying here in this van with him for weeks sounded like heaven. "You're sure Herman can hold two of us?"

He grinned. "I'm sure. But you know the draw-backs—tiny toilet, no shower, decided lack of gourmet cooking." He frowned at the milk in the pot.

"Sponge baths haven't been bad so far. And the cooking might not be gourmet, but the view's all right."

Naked with the pot in one hand, Blake laughed. "I'll have to get an apron for safety's sake." He wrinkled his nose. "Sorry, I think this milk is singed."

"You'll have to come back to bed and warm up be-fore we go to the house."

Kicking off his moccasins, Blake climbed back under the covers with me and nuzzled my cheek, his lips tender. "It's the smart thing to do before braving the elements."

As we moved closer, our legs tangling and mouths meeting, Ella leapt between us with a thump, shoving her muzzle into our faces.

"Your protector is, well, dogged," Blake said, squirm-ing and turning his head.

"Nice one."

"I'm a writer, after all."

"About that—tell me one of your stories?"

As Ella settled between us, a smile lifted Blake's lips. "Okay. Just one before we go. It starts on a space station two-point-five million light years away in the galaxy of Andromeda."

Safe and warm under the covers with Ella soon snoring softly, I listened to Blake's story and dreamed of the future.

Chapter Seven

Blake

"SANTA CLAUS IS Comin' to Town" rang out above the din of chattering voices and shrieks of children's laughter outside the barn and across the yard. The kids waiting for Santa were pumped up on intensely sweet maple candies from Nadeau's, a nearby maple syrup farm Nick and Hunter partnered with that was family owned and operated.

The son, Max, had dropped off syrup and candies with his boyfriend, an adorable redheaded twink with glasses. I'd never have expected Pinevale to become a queer hotspot, but here we were. Maybe we should start a club.

Because I wasn't going anywhere.

I dissolved another maple candy in my mouth and watched Caleb across the barn's rear storage area. His break was over, and he was getting ready to face the hordes once more. I'd come through the back door to catch a minute with him before I supervised the next tree-cutting expedition, but I'd stopped in my tracks to watch him unawares.

Beyond the stacks of boxes and crates, he moaned softly, and my eyes were glued to the arch of his back, the fake belly protruding. Arms high, he grasped one wrist and stretched to the side. Then the other, a soft little noise of exertion drifting over to me.

He'd been grunting a *lot* louder earlier in bed, the world still winter-dark when we woke in each other's arms and got sweaty under the duvet. Then on top of it. Who needed a heater when you had the sexiest man in the world? Santa's beard and belly somehow made me want him more.

I jerked to attention at the sound of a low whistle beside me. I hadn't heard Hunter's approach, and now he gave me what could only be described as a shit-eating grin. Shifting the box of craft supplies in his arms, he whistled again.

"Got it bad, don't you? Looks like you're about to march over there and strip him right out of that Santa suit." Hunter leaned in closer. "I'd lend you my sexy elf costume, but it's too small even for me. No way it would fit you."

I huffed and tried to laugh it off, my ears burning and face undoubtedly as red as said Santa suit. "I'm not—we're—" My laugh was a painful little *ha-ha-haaaaa.*

Hunter still grinned. "Nothing wrong with a little holiday fling."

I shrugged, my face burning beet/cherry/tomato/fire engine red—take your pick. But my pleasure and embarrassment faded. *Holiday fling.* It had been impossible to hide that Caleb was staying with me in Herman since his pickup was parked by the house, so of course Hunter and Nick knew we were fucking.

Fling.

It was a reasonable assumption. But it made my skin feel too tight.

Hunter's smirk transformed into a frown. He bent to deposit the box at his feet before straightening. "What's up?" He propped a hip on the nearby workbench, clearly ready to listen.

I'd been his TA at university, but we'd never been close friends or anything. He and Nick had given me work and a free place to park my van when I wanted it the past couple of years, and we were certainly friendly. But we'd never discussed anything particularly deep or personal.

"Nothing. How's the patient?"

Hunter's smile was undeniably affectionate. "Healing right on schedule after surgery. That break was definitely not going to mend without a screw put in. Although the patient still has to *be* patient. Not his best event, although I suspect he's secretly glad he can hide away in the house and get out of playing Santa."

"I bet."

Hunter glanced to Caleb, who straightened his beard and slipped back out of the storage area to the main part of the barn. Excited cries from waiting children rose to the rafters.

"Caleb's really stepped up," Hunter said. "We're going to hire him on in the new year. The major work won't start until spring, but there'll be enough to do, especially with Nick recovering."

"That's great!" Caleb really was an excellent worker, and a permanent job would relieve so much of his stress.

"It is. So, what's eating you?" Hunter asked.

What the hell. Before I could change my mind, I said, "The thing is, we actually knew each other in high school."

"Ah. Nick mentioned there was a weird vibe when he introduced you."

"Yeah. I guess I was in denial. It was a hell of a shock to come face to face with him after all this time. It ended badly. Well…abruptly. He just never spoke to me again."

Hunter winced. "Crap. After you two…" He swirled his hand through the air.

"Yeah. We finally got together one night. He promised he was going to break up with his girlfriend and all that stuff. I wasn't out at school, but I was at home. Anyway, he just never talked to me again. Never even *looked* at me. There were only a few weeks of school left, so that was just…it."

"Wow. That sucks."

"Yeah. And I know he's sorry. He's apologized. We did talk about it, and then we—" My turn to motion with my hand.

Hunter's mouth tugged into a smaller version of his shit-eating grin. "Thank god for blizzards, am I right?"

I had to smile. "Indeed."

"Okay. What's got you so serious? I assume you two are having a good time. You sure seem to be."

"Definitely." I wasn't typically the shy sort, but my face was just going to be permanently red at this point. It was different talking about Caleb for some reason.

For some reason. I scoffed at myself. *Gee, I wonder why, my guy?*

Hunter said, "He was the one who got away."

"I guess so." I crossed and uncrossed my arms, then crossed them again. "Not exactly." I took a deep breath and slowly blew it out. "He was the one who broke my heart."

Mouth pinched in sympathy, Hunter was about to say something when his gaze shifted. His spine went rigid. "Hey, Caleb!"

I spun to find Caleb hovering nearby. Clearly close enough to overhear. His eyes were wide above the fluffy beard, the fur-trimmed hat pulled low. My heart thudded as he cleared his throat.

"Um, sorry. The music's stuck."

Hunter cursed. "That old CD player of Nick's." He glanced to me. "Let me go fix it and entertain the kids for a few minutes. Ella can help distract them. Santa can take a break and you two can talk." He gave my arm a squeeze and hurried away.

Caleb and I faced each other. I hadn't noticed it before, but the sound of "Deck the Halls" skipping on the "fa-la-la-la-la" echoed through the barn before being silenced.

I took another deep breath. "Well. Yeah, so. You did break my heart back then."

He nodded. "I'm sorry."

"I know you are. I believe you. I—" A half laugh escaped. "Can you take off the beard? It's weird having this conversation with Santa."

Laughing nervously, he tugged off the hat and beard, dropping them on the table. Hands at his sides, he fidgeted, his fingers twitching.

"Even after you broke my heart, I never stopped loving you." The words didn't come easily, but I said them, slow and steady and honest. "I want more than a holiday fling. I want to know you again. I want to see if we can make it work. Make it last. What would you say if I don't go south for the winter? If I moved in with you at the cottage. Helped you fix it up. I can write in Herman if I need my own space."

"What would I say?" He gaped at me. "You're the one who's good with words. I'd just say hell yes. Let's do it."

We moved at the same time, arms around each other, mouths eager. Santa's fake belly bounced between us, keeping our lower bodies apart as we kissed deeply. I laughed as I gasped for air, and Caleb grinned.

"Probably for the best with a barn full of children right out there," I muttered. "I shouldn't be debauching Santa."

"Not until later," he whispered, biting his lip.

"Mmm. Food for thought." I kissed him again softly before smacking his ass. "Now find out who's been naughty or nice. You'll have to ask me tonight."

With a snort-laugh, Caleb put on his beard and straightened the belly. He was at the door when he rushed back. "Wait. Did I say I love you too? Because I do. I did then. I do now."

My heart soared as I kissed him, silly Santa beard and all.

"Sorry!" Hunter called out, wincing. "These kids are going to riot if Santa doesn't come back."

Wiping his mouth, Caleb nodded, looking anywhere but at Hunter. Then something seemed to occur to him, and he stopped in his tracks. "I guess you know I'm gay."

Hunter nodded seriously. "We did figure it out when you started sleeping over in Blake's tiny van."

"Herman's not tiny!" I insisted. "He's mid-sized."

Ignoring me, which was fair, Hunter told Caleb, "You're welcome here. And safe. Actually, we'd love to hire you full time. I'll draw up a contract after the holiday madness is over. Assuming you're still interested?"

"Yes!" Caleb shouted, then cleared his throat. "Yes. Thank you."

A swell of children's impatient cries rose, and Caleb shot me a grin. I wanted to kiss him again so much it hurt, but it could wait. We didn't need to rush.

As we climbed out of his truck, Caleb groaned. "I ate too much turkey. And ham. And stuffing."

"Don't forget the roast potatoes," I said. My jeans were definitely snug after Christmas dinner the night before with Nick, Hunter, Hunter's mom, and a few other people. I reached back into the truck. "And don't forget your skates. You'll need those last time I checked, though you're the hockey expert."

Fists jammed in his coat pockets, he scoffed. "I haven't played in years."

"You'll be the belle of the ball if I remember your stick-handling." I glanced around the arena's parking lot, which was about half full, families trickling out as the free skating time came to an end. No one was in earshot. "I'm a big fan of how you handle my stick."

Instead of snort-laughing, Caleb only glanced at the arena as though it was the last place he wanted to go. He fiddled with his scarf, tightening it so much he'd strangle himself.

"Okay," I said. "What's up? That was a quality pun you ignored. Fine, the quality is debatable, but what's going on in that pretty head of yours?"

He flushed below his beard to the tips of his ears, a

pleased smile tugging his lips. I made a mental note to call him "pretty" more often. I asked softly, "What are you so nervous about?"

"I haven't played in years. I'm beyond rusty."

"Yeah, but your knee's okay, right? It'll be like riding a bike."

"I dunno."

"No one will expect you to be the captain out there. There's no pressure. They don't know you."

He sighed, untying the scarf and pulling the ends until they hung evenly around his neck. "That's part of it. They don't know me, and I'm not sure how to… Get to know them."

"Well, I realize you were overseas for quite a while, but it is our custom here to say 'hi' and shake hands. Or perhaps 'hello' and a nod if you're feeling standoffish."

"Ha ha. I mean… I want to get to know them the right way."

"The right way?"

"The *honest* way. So they know who I am. No hiding."

"Ah."

"Am I supposed to walk in and say, 'Hi, I'm Caleb, and I'm gay'? No one does that. I don't know how to be out. I don't know how to join a hockey league and tell everyone I'm gay."

"It's not as if you need to march in and do a '*hear-ye, hear-ye*' announcement. You can tell people when you're ready."

"But when will that be? What if I just end up hiding all over again? I'm afraid I'll do it all wrong. Again. I want…" He took a deep, shuddering breath. "I want to be brave."

My heart clenched. "Do you trust me?"

"Yes." He nodded seriously.

"Then we'd better get in there."

The arena lobby smelled of grease and cheap lemon cleaner. We pushed through the main doors to the rink, the temperature dropping instantly. With our fingers laced together, I squeezed his sweaty palm.

One of the guys lacing his skates on the bench by the ice glanced over. His gaze dropped for a moment to our linked hands, then back up. He smiled as he stood and stuck out his hand. "Hey, I'm Tony. Any preference on position?"

With an incredible display of fortitude, I resisted making a pun.

Epilogue

Caleb

Two Years Later

THROUGH THE THINNING trees, I spotted home. We'd strung the colored Christmas lights along the eaves of the original cottage and the addition that doubled its size.

The new truck's engine purred as I parked it beside Herman, and my butt was toasty from the built-in seat warmer. Blake had been right—it was worth the upgrade.

As I climbed down, bracing in the icy wind, snow crunching under my boots, Poppy raced out, barking with pure joy. I inhaled the woodsmoke that meant Blake had the stove going.

I crouched to greet Poppy, scratching behind her floppy ears. We weren't sure which breeds her parents had been, but her ears reminded us of Ella, who was still going strong.

"Did you miss me?" I murmured to Poppy. "I missed you too, darling."

"What about me?" Blake asked from the new covered porch, shivering in the wind, his feet shoved into boots. "I missed you. Granted, I've never pissed myself because I'm *that* excited you're home again. Poppy will always have one up on me."

I snorted and pocketed the truck's keys. "How did the chapter go?"

He shrugged. "Okay. Maybe? Hard to tell sometimes. I made the butternut squash casserole for the potluck tomorrow night."

"I'm sure the chapter's great. And thanks for doing that." I squinted past the cottage and across the lake. "Dawn and Logan went all out, huh?"

"Those halls are officially decked," Blake agreed. "Are you driving to hockey with him in the morning? I wanted to run a few errands."

"Yeah, he'll swing by and get me."

"Speaking of decking the halls, we should get a tree before the good ones are gone."

I walked around to the back of the truck and lowered the tailgate. "Hope this one will do."

Blake appeared at my side, and he made a show of inspecting the silver fir. "Well, I may be an ex-lumberjack—at least for now since I'm working on this new series—but it looks perfect. Not too tall for your mom's angel to go on top?"

"Should be just right."

Shivering in his thin sweater, Blake leaned close and kissed me, our beards scraping. Without needing to speak, we hauled the tree just like we used to, the movements second nature.

Later, with burgers grilling on the porch and sweet potato fries in the air fryer, I looked up at the golden angel—which had a good foot of clearance under the timber ceiling. Poppy snored by our feet, and Blake wrapped his arms around me from behind, nuzzling my neck.

There were times I got down on myself for how many years I'd wasted when Blake and I could have been together. But who knew what would have happened back then? I was brave now, and we had a home.

Everything was just right.

THE END

About the Author

Keira aims for the perfect mix of character, plot, and heat in her M/M romances. She writes everything from swashbuckling pirates to heartwarming holiday escapism. Her fave tropes are enemies to lovers, age gaps, forced proximity, and passionate virgins. Although she loves delicious angst along the way, Keira guarantees happy endings!

Discover more at:

keiraandrews.com

Printed in Great Britain
by Amazon

32975925R00067